I0761932

THE SWORDSMAN'S LAMENT

THE ROYAL CHAMPION

BOOK 1

G.M. WHITE

TWIN STAR PRESS

The Swordsman's Lament
G.M. White

Editor: Vicky Brewster
Cover design: Get Covers

AUTHOR'S NOTE ON SPELLINGS (AND AI)

Please note, the author is British, and so uses British English spellings throughout.

No AI was used in the writing of this book, it is the work of a human mind with all the frailties and faults that entails.

1

It was a little after lunch, and Belasko had already killed three men. He frowned at their bodies, scattered across the duelling circle which had been crudely scratched into the dirt of the street. He should have expected that his challenger had friends that wanted in on the act, but didn't expect them to break the rules and jump in all at once. Was nothing sacred anymore?

He touched his brow. It was as he'd said inside; he'd killed them without breaking a sweat. He flexed his foot. It was the damnable ache that slowed him, made his thrusts weaker, as he couldn't push off properly. These three, these boys, had got closer than anyone should, and all because of the pain in his foot. He sighed before turning to wave at the gathered crowd. He really was getting older.

Thirty-seven wasn't old by the standards of Villanese society, but it was old for a duellist. You don't see many old duellists, or retired ones, because there will always come someone who wants to challenge you. To build their reputation on your own. Worse still for the king's champion. No shortage of challengers for him.

All I wanted was a bite to eat and some peace and quiet, Belasko thought, *not to kill three stupid boys. Still, it was a damn fine meal...* He snorted. *And I thought I wouldn't be recognised in this part of town.*

Belasko nursed his beer and looked around the inn. It was busy, a mix of people from different classes filling the public dining and taproom. Labourers dressed in rough cloth jostled for space on communal benches, whereas prosperous merchants paid extra for private tables. It was a middling sort of place, but he preferred those to the finer establishments the city had to offer. Less chance of recognition and the challenges that often followed. Still, the meal had been surprisingly good and the ale was very fine. When the innkeeper brought his bill, he tried to guess the worth of the food and drink he had just enjoyed.

He smiled at the older man, a stout fellow who was greying at the temples. An honest face hovered above the innkeeper's uniform of sturdy work clothes covered by an ever-present apron, shirtsleeves rolled up to the elbow, the harried look of the permanently busy about him. Belasko smiled and covered the bill with his hand.

"Now, my good man, before I look at the bill you've brought me, let me tell you that that was as fine a meal as I've eaten in any establishment in this city — and I've eaten at some of the very best. Before I leave, may I pay my compliments to the chef?"

The innkeeper coloured at the praise. "Kendra!" he bellowed over his shoulder before turning to smile at Belasko. "Thank you, sir, that is praise indeed. I know she's a good cook and all—"

They were interrupted by a young woman who came bustling out of the kitchens, wiping her hands on her apron.

"What is it? If it's another—" She stopped short at the sight of Belasko and the smiling innkeeper. "Oh, sorry. How can I be of assistance?"

The innkeeper gestured at Belasko. "The gentleman here was just being very complimentary about the food and asked to meet the chef before he leaves."

"Kendra, was it? I..." Belasko paused, noticing the similarities between the innkeeper and the cook. "Your daughter?" he asked the innkeeper, who nodded. "You must be very proud. Kendra, the meal I have just eaten was simply delicious. The seasoning both delicate and exquisite. You have a rare gift." He looked at the innkeeper. "I must say, the beer is very fine too."

Belasko tapped his fingers on the bill the innkeeper had brought him. "Here's what I'd like to do. I'll put down what I think the meal is worth before I look at the bill. If the bill is for less, you keep the difference with my compliments; if it is higher then accept my apologies, and I'll reach into my purse again."

The innkeeper frowned but nodded, clearly unsure.

"Now, as I said, that was as fine a meal as I've eaten in this city, and I've eaten in establishments both low and high. I've dined at the palace on more than one occasion. Elsewhere in the city, I would happily pay, oh, four crowns and a stag." He laid the coins out on the table. The innkeeper's face paled at the sight of the money. "Now let's look at the bill." Belasko turned it over, read the amount written, and laughed. He slid the coins over to the innkeeper. "You, sir, are seriously undercharging. Please, take these with my compliments."

While the innkeeper and his daughter blushed at the praise, and insisted that he accept the change he was due, Belasko smiled. He liked to tip generously when he could, and the meal really had been that good.

His purse strings were a little tighter than normal, having taken a loan to acquire more land for the academy. They needed better access to water and their own logging rights if they were to get through another winter as fierce as the last. Some wondered why a man at his station in life would resort to a loan, but while Belasko's star rode high in Villanese society, he put most of his money into the Academy and his students. When all was said and done, they were his legacy.

"No, no, please take the money. The meal was worth it. You really need to start charging more. Be careful, though. I hear the palace is looking for a new cook and they might poach Kendra right out from under you. If I didn't have a good cook on my staff already I know I'd be tempted."

Belasko was interrupted by a heavy hand on his shoulder. *Bugger. Recognised. Here it comes.*

"Here, ain't you that duellist? Greatest swordsman in the world or some shit?"

He stood and turned, chair screeching against the flagstones, throwing the hand off his shoulder and pushing back the man it belonged to in one smooth motion.

"Am I Belasko, most gifted with a blade? Hero of Dellan Pass? Never defeated in the duelling circle? The king's personal champion? Yes. Greatest swordsman in the world? I've yet to meet better, but in truth it's a young man's game and I'm no longer young."

"You don't look that old either," Kendra said from over his shoulder.

Belasko smiled at her. "That's very kind of you, but every year I get a little slower, relying more on skill, technique and experience than speed. I've yet to meet my better, but one day that will come." He pursed his lips and eyed the young man that had recognised him, taking in his ragged clothing, the sword at his hip that although worn and battered through use, looked ill cared for. "But I think it is not today."

The rest of the inn, which had gone deathly silent at the

prospect of a challenge, stirred into laughter at this. The man who had accosted Belasko flushed.

Good. Anger. Anything that will put you out of balance, Belasko thought. He turned to the room.

"Mind you, have you lot not heard the swordsman's lament?"

"No," came a voice from the crowd, "what's that?"

Belasko grinned. "The older I get, the better I was."

The crowd laughed louder at this and Belasko turned again to the man who had recognised him. "Are you sure you'd like to put me to the test, sir? While I might be getting older—" He flexed his left foot in his boot. The pain wasn't too bad today. "—I could still kill you and any other man in here without breaking a sweat." He smiled apologetically at the innkeeper and his daughter. "Not that I would. I would hate to spoil a very pleasant afternoon, or do any damage to your establishment. If this young idiot insists on throwing his life away, we'll take it outside."

He looked back at the man he knew he'd soon be fighting, noting that his insults had hit home. Belasko sighed and rolled his shoulders, freeing them up for what was to come.

"So, what is it to be? Will you challenge, or can I go back to enjoying my afternoon in peace?"

The young man drew himself up to his not unimpressive height. *Damn, he's tall. He'll have a better reach than me.* He sneered at Belasko, hawked and spat on the inn floor. "I challenge," he hissed from between his teeth.

Belasko sighed, before reaching into his purse and flicking another coin to the innkeeper. "Please, for the young man's rudeness and the inconvenience."

The innkeeper swallowed. "Inconvenience? When word gets out that Belasko fought a duel outside, our business will double."

Belasko smiled. "Then I wish you well of it." He turned back to his challenger, who had somehow managed to flush darker still and was almost purple with rage. "Oh yes, you. I accept. Shall we go outside?"

~

Ah well, another tale to add to the legend. By the time the story of this afternoon's little adventure has spread three streets away, the number of attackers will have doubled. By the time it's reached the next quarter, they'll have tripled.

Belasko leaned down, wiping the blood from his blade on the shirt of his fallen challenger before sheathing it in the scabbard he wore at his hip. A rapier, light and ideal for duelling, he always wore it about town.

"Excuse me, Mr Belasko? Sir?" Belasko looked up. It was the innkeeper.

Belasko smiled and clapped him on the shoulder. "Just Belasko is fine, and apologies again for this incident. It's a hazard of my trade I'm afraid. I'm sorry, I didn't take your name?"

The innkeeper blinked. "Kander, sir — I mean, Belasko. My name is Kander."

"Kander. I am sorry about this mess outside your establishment. No doubt the constables are already on their way to clear up. Ah, here they come now." The sounds of whistles in the distance heralded the arrival of the city watch. Belasko would apologise to them when they arrived, both for the mess and for having them stirred from their watch house.

Kander smiled. "Please, don't apologise. If people don't know better than to challenge the king's champion then they deserve what they get." He frowned. "Particularly when they break the rules of the circle. I couldn't believe it when the other two jumped in. That would never have happened in my day." The innkeeper shook his head. "A sign of the times."

"Your day? Were you a duellist?" *I should have known, he carries himself well.*

Kander laughed. "Oh no, sir — I mean, Belasko — not a duellist. I was a soldier in another life and we occasionally settled differences in the circle. Just to first blood, or they'd have had us hanged."

"That sounds like the wisdom of commanding officers: 'If you kill each other we'll hang you!' I was a soldier myself before — well, you know."

"I do. We all do. I doubt there's anyone in the country that doesn't know your story. Listen, can I offer you a drink? On the house. You've already overpaid for your meal, I couldn't charge you more."

Belasko looked around at the dispersing crowd. The street was already returning to its normal background hubbub, people taking care not to disturb the duelling circle and the bodies within as they made their way past and in and out of the nearby businesses. He shook his head. "I'd love to, Kander, but once word gets out about this challenge others will come. More idiots looking to make their mark. I'd best be getting home."

"I understand." Kander squinted at Belasko. "What you said before, about the palace kitchens, them needing a chef. Is that true? Only..." The innkeeper sighed. "My Kendra's too good for the inn. I can't charge what her food's worth, not in this part of town, and although it would hurt me to lose her I just want the best for my girl. She deserves her chance to shine. To show what she can do."

Belasko nodded. "It's true, and from what I've sampled she'd be more than up to the task. Would you like me to have a word, put her name forward?"

"Oh, if you could, that would be wonderful. Thank you!"

"In fact, I'll do better than that. Do you by any chance have private dining rooms?"

"Oh yes, several."

"Well, keep the grandest one you have free for me tomorrow night. I'll return to sample her cooking with some people who are best placed to make the decision. Just don't let on to anyone that I'm coming back, or that I'm bringing guests with me. Can you do that?"

Kander grinned. "Can I? Of course I can! Thank you so much, I honestly can't thank you enough. Oh, can I tell Kendra? Just so she can make something special."

"Of course, but no one else. Keep it secret, alright? We'll come to the back door, so as not to advertise our presence." Belasko reached out his hand and the two men clasped wrists, shaking on the deal.

"You know what's responsible for too much death? More than you'd think?" Maelyn, the royal physician, looked up from her examination of Belasko's left foot. A diminutive woman with steel grey hair, a fierce intelligence shone out of her piercing blue eyes. Her slight build belied a surprising strength.

"No, but I'm sure you'll enlighten me."

The next day found Belasko in the physician's suite at the palace, her treatment room to be precise. It was a functional room with several couches and treatment tables, the charts and illustrations of human anatomy hung on the walls the only decoration. A faint aroma from the remedies Maelyn prepared and dispensed hung in the air. He was stripped to his small-clothes sitting on a low couch, as Maelyn examined his bad foot and other joints.

"Pride. Damnable, pig-headed pride. Whether that's the pride that brings armies to battle—" Belasko winced as the physician probed the joints of his foot. "—or the pride that keeps someone from visiting their doctor so they then die of a curable illness. That last one is usually the preserve of men.

You're from farming stock, aren't you? They're often the worst. Work themselves into the grave while their body falls apart, but mustn't grumble. Mustn't complain. Right." The little physician sat back and clapped her hands. "On with your clothes."

"So, what do you think?" Belasko asked as he shrugged on his shirt.

Maelyn's eyebrows rose. "What do I think? I think you have a problem that's not going to get any better."

Belasko reached for his breeches. "I know that, but will it get worse?"

The little physician sighed. "Yes, I'm afraid so. There are a few things you can do that should alleviate the pain and stiffness in your other joints, but I'm afraid the damage to your foot is permanent. It will only get worse. You've pushed your body hard over the years, and it's coming back to haunt you. It's rare to see such ailments in someone your age, but not unheard of. Tell me, have either of your parents had similar problems?"

"I don't know. I haven't seen them in years."

"I see."

Belasko cleared his throat. "What can I do, then? Anything?"

Maelyn pursed her lips. "You're already doing most of what can be done. Exercise is good, gets the blood flowing, and you do plenty of that. Try to keep to things that won't place too much impact on the joints — that's probably how you got into this state in the first place. Swimming is good, particularly in cold water. I think you said you had somewhere suitable on the grounds of your academy?"

Belasko nodded. "Yes, there's a small lake. More of a large pond, really. It's deep enough for swimming, bloody cold too."

"Good. Try to swim in it regularly. Avoid exercises that will jar your joints, such as, oh I don't know, banging bloody great lengths of steel together."

"Nice try. You know I can't do that. I need to keep training, both for my students and my own sake. I still get challenged, you know."

Maelyn frowned. "Yes, I heard about your little adventure yesterday. What was it, three at once?"

"It was only supposed to be one, then his friends joined in."

The physician sighed. "You no doubt dispatched them with style and aplomb. Let me ask you, though: how close did they get? I heard it was three unschooled boys that should have known better. How close?"

Belasko paused in the act of pulling on one of his boots. Then, quiet, "Too close. They got too close."

Maelyn leaned over and patted him on the shoulder. "You might be the best, my boy, but age comes to us all. There's no harm in getting out while you still can. Why not retire?"

"Don't you know, Doctor, there are no retired duellists? Only dead ones." Belasko shook his head. "Besides, I can't retire yet. I've too much to do. A replacement to find and train up."

"And how long have you been looking, my boy? How many years? You'll not find another like you. You're a rare breed. A legend, or so they tell me. You might just have to settle for someone that can do the job."

"When I find someone who can do the job as well as I can, that's when I'll retire."

The physician laughed. "I'll believe it when I see it. Now, off with you. I'll make up something to help with the pain in your foot and have it sent over to your house. Where are you off to now?"

Belasko stood, straightening his collar. "I have dinner plans."

Across town, Kander was fretting around his daughter in the kitchen. A hot, busy room, clouds of steam and the smell of cooking food filled the air. With staff bustling in and out, Kendra ruled over the kitchen from her position between the ovens and the open fireplace. She frowned, swatting her father's hands away from a cooking pot with a wooden spoon.

"Come now, Father, there's no need to be nervous. The duellist already said he liked our food. What more do we have to prove?"

Kander wrung his hands, uncharacteristically anxious. "It's just the people he's bringing with him, they'll decide whether you get taken on at the palace kitchens. Isn't that something to be nervous about?"

Kendra gave her father a stony look. "You know I'm happy here. If these guests are impressed by my cooking and offer me a job at the palace, then that's wonderful. If they don't, that's fine too. It's not like I've lost anything if I don't get offered the job. Besides, who'll look after little Albin if I go up to the palace?" Her son, at five years old, was a handful. Between Kendra, her father, and the other staff at the inn, they managed to care for him and keep him mostly out of trouble. As she looked at her father her expression softened and she leaned forward to place a kiss on his brow. "I suppose we'll sort things out if it comes to that. Now look, you fretting in here is putting me off. Let me get on with what I do best, and you get ready to welcome our guests. And make sure not to forget about our regulars in the common room in the process."

Kander threw his hands up. "Alright, alright, I know when I'm not wanted." He winked at her to soften his words. "I'll go and busy myself in the common room until they arrive."

He went out, leaving Kendra to her work. She frowned, tapping a finger on her lips. "Now, where did I put that Aruvian pepper?"

As they approached the back door to the inn, Belasko murmured to his companions, "Best let me knock and exchange pleasantries before we go in. We don't want our little escort to alarm anyone."

He walked down the back street accompanied by three figures, all cloaked and hooded against the evening's chill, and a small company of guards in plain livery but well-made armour — functional, not flashy. Belasko himself was dressed in well-made doublet and hose in muted colours, careless of the increasing cold, with a short cape thrown nonchalantly over one shoulder to leave his sword arm free, and knee-high riding boots on his feet. Their footsteps clattered on the cobbles and echoed off the surrounding buildings, mingling with the occasional clink of armour and creak of leather, before being lost in the general hubbub of the city at night.

The taller of the three hooded forms waved his hand in the air. "Whatever you say Belasko, I'm sure we're happy to follow your lead. Just let's not be too long about supper, I have a function I need to get to later this evening."

A snort came from under one of the other's hoods, followed by a wry voice. "A 'function', is it? Another one of your revelries I'm sure. Still, if the food Belasko's promised us is as good as he says then you'll be well set up for an evening of carousing."

The third, shortest and slight of build, remained silent.

Once again I play the mediator. "Come now gentlemen, no need for argument. Let us enjoy our dinner. Debate is best made on a full stomach. Over brandy. Ah, here we are." Belasko stepped up to the stout back door of the inn, the muted sounds of its inhabitants and their own evening's revelries drifting down to them from high windows. He rapped firmly on the door three times.

There followed a few quiet moments, then the sound of bolts being thrown back before the door was heaved open and Kander, blinking out at the dark, stood before them.

"Belasko! Welcome, welcome. You're just in time. Do come in."

Belasko reached out and clasped the inn keeper's hand. "Good to see you again, Kander. Do you mind if a few of our men have a quick look inside first? Just to check the dining room, you understand."

Kander peered out, taking in Belasko's companions and retinue. He swallowed. The number of guards and the quality of their armour spoke volumes about the wealth and importance of the guests he would be hosting. "Of—of course I don't mind. Please, gentlemen, this way. Let me show you through to the dining room, it's the finest we have..." Kander's voice faded as he led several of the guards down the corridor.

"Tell me, what do we know of this innkeeper?" asked Belasko's second companion, their wry tone replaced with curiosity.

Belasko shrugged. "Once a soldier, seems a good sort. His daughter is an exceptionally talented cook. What more do you need to know?"

His companion laughed. "You would never have made an intelligence operative, Belasko. There's always more to any situation than meets the eye, and I like to know as much as I can about the people I meet."

Belasko grinned, patting the rapier at his side. "It's a good thing you don't keep me around for my intelligence then, isn't it?"

All his companions laughed at this, the tallest reaching out to clap him on the shoulder. "Never mind old man, you have many redeeming qualities, I'm sure. Do let us know when you find out what they are."

Belasko raised an eyebrow. "'Old man'? Less of that, if you please. I'm only a few years older than you and could still best you every day of the week, twice on feast days ."

His third companion spoke at last, a female voice. "Really

gentlemen, is this what passes for wit in the company of men? I should have stayed at home with my books, at least they're reliably entertaining."

They all laughed again just as their guard returned with Kander. They nodded, apparently satisfied with the arrangements inside.

"Right then," Belasko said, pointing at guards as he spoke, "two of you stay out here to mind the door, two come to watch the stairs — the dining room is upstairs, isn't it Kander?" The inn keeper nodded. "Good. Two more to guard the door to the dining room. The rest of you, disperse but don't go far. Keep an eye on the entrances and exits. It might be an idea to have a few men in the common room, but watch what you drink. You're still on duty."

The guardsmen peeled off to their assignments and Belasko and his companions followed Kander into the inn.

The innkeeper led them into a sumptuously decorated private dining room, with deep carpets and intricately detailed tapestries on the walls. The furniture was expensive, dark hard wood polished until it gleamed, and there were curios and decorations of excellent craftsmanship on stands and in cabinets around the walls. Pride of place was given to the large dining table and chairs in the centre of the room.

Belasko whistled. "Kander, you surprise me. This is fine indeed."

Kander shrugged. "I know we might not be in the best part of town, but I like to aim high. Word of Kendra's skill in the kitchen has got around. We get the occasional noble or lord merchant coming to dine. Might as well make them feel welcome."

One of Belasko's companions moved to the table, where

four places were set, and took the place at its head. "Never mind nobles or lord merchants my good Kander, I'd say your dining room is fit for a king." He drew back the hood of his cloak, revealing himself to be a fine-featured older man, with salt and pepper beard and hair, and a sardonic smile. Clad in a black and gold brocade doublet, richly embroidered with the royal house's silver stag, a gold circlet sat on his brow.

The taller companion, at his right hand side, drew back his own hood. "And maybe for his son as well." A handsome man in his early thirties, he had dark hair, the flushed complexion of a seasoned drinker, and a self-satisfied grin. His doublet was equally fine, of scarlet and gold, depicting satyrs chasing dancing nymphs. He wore a silver circlet.

"Let's not forget his daughter, shall we?" At this the third companion drew back her hood, revealing herself to be a young woman, fine featured with golden hair that was artfully entwined around her own silver circlet. She wore a gown of deceptively simply cut, with white and gold panels, tightly laced across the bodice and trimmed with fur at the cuffs and hems. A playful smile hovered about her lips, threatening to break out at any time.

Kander gawped at the three of them.

As different as they make out they are, they all enjoy this sort of thing, Belasko thought. "Well," he said aloud, "I did tell you I'd bring people who were best placed to decide who gets employed in the palace kitchens. Who better than the most important people that would be eating the food?"

Kander swallowed, gathered himself, and offered a deep bow. First to the man wearing the gold circlet, then the man and woman in silver. "King Mallor, your majesty. Your highnesses Prince Kellan, Princess Lilliana, I had no idea... My humble house is honoured. I'm sorry, Belasko didn't tell me..."

King Mallor smiled gently. "Peace, honourable innkeeper. It

is good that he didn't. We have to keep such excursions outside the palace walls quiet, for safety's sake."

"Also we'll get a much more honest sample of your daughter's cooking this way. Although if Belasko's word is true then we've nothing to fear on that account," said Prince Kellan. He coughed. "Now, would there be anything in the way of refreshment?"

Kander clasped his hands together. "Of course your highness, I have an excellent Cantrian red that I've been saving for a special occasion. Or would you prefer some of our beer? Brewed to my family's recipe."

"The beer is very good," Belasko said. "Definitely worth a try."

"I tell you what, good innkeeper, how about we each have a flagon of your beer to start and then wine with our meal?" said the king.

"Of course your majesty. Please, make yourselves comfortable. I'll bring the beer and then tell you the menu for the evening."

"Excellent. Oh, and Kander? Don't tell your daughter who your guests are. Not yet. We wouldn't want to put her off."

"Whatever's the matter, Father?" Kendra asked as Kander appeared in the kitchen. "You're sweating. Who's the swordsman brought with him to get you in such a state?"

Kander blinked at his daughter as he mopped his brow. "Oh, no one, no one... Just some important people from the palace. They've asked for some beer before dinner, which I'm to take them now. What have you cooked for them? Just so I can give them the menu."

Kendra gave her father a wicked grin. "Oh, I've something special for them. Plain, honest fair, the sort that they're probably crying out for at the palace. You can only take so many stuffed larks' tongues, you know."

"Wicked child, you'll be the death of me. You know this is your chance to impress these people. Important people."

Kendra frowned. "Yes, you've said. Well, Belasko praised my seasoning, which got me thinking. I'm making a deceptively plain menu, hearty but delicious. Just three courses. A country vegetable soup to start, venison stew for the main, poached pears for dessert."

Kander swallowed. "Very good, very good. I'll just take the beer up and let them know."

"You might as well pull on the Water King's beard as try to find a truly peaceful Baskan," Prince Kellan said. "Why? Because a peaceful Baskan no more exists than the bogeyman the common people say lives down by the docks."

His father sighed and shook his head at the mention of the mythical figure. "Well, with the trouble we've been having along the southern border I fear we may be heading towards war once more, despite out best efforts to come to peaceful terms in recent years."

Prince Kellan snorted. "Those bloody Baskan upstarts, they—"

"Are just doing what our own ancestors did, long ago," his sister interrupted. "Which you'd know if you'd paid attention to old Eade's history lessons."

"That pompous fart, how anyone could listen to him without falling asleep I don't know."

"You certainly did that often enough, otherwise you might have learned a thing or two."

King Mallor laughed. "Peace my children, peace. Kellan, Lilliana is quite right. Please, my dear, expand on the subject for your wayward brother." Kellan flushed as Lilliana continued.

"Thank you, Father. You see, brother, hundreds of years ago we were just like the Baskans. A young nation looking to expand, taking land and wealth from others. If we hadn't been as the Baskans are now, we would still be ruling over a small fortified settlement on the island where our palace stands. We never had much cause to worry about our neighbours to the south, a ragtag collection of squabbling city states and principalities too busy fighting amongst each other to cause us any bother. But then..."

"They stopped squabbling, and unified under one dominant house." King Mallor's face was grim now. "Unified whether they liked it or not. They've been a single nation for all of two generations and, as Lilliana says, started looking to expand. Which brought them into conflict with us in the Last War, in which Belasko here acquitted himself so well and helped keep the Baskans back."

Belasko inclined his head towards the king, accepting the compliment. "Thank you, your majesty, although it took the effort and lives of a great many men and women to push the Baskan forces back." He leaned forward, resting his elbows on the table. "I'm curious to know why you think we might be at risk of another war."

King Mallor frowned and began to speak, before pausing at a knock on the door, followed by Kander bustling in with a tray of beers in his hands. He set about serving them, placing the flagons on the table. The king reached out, picked up his flagon, and took a sip. He made an appreciative face. "My dear Kander, this is very fine indeed. Never mind your daughter working in the kitchens, could I induce you to come work in my brew house?"

Kander smiled. "That's very kind of your majesty. It's a

family recipe, as I said, and I think it as fine a beer as you'll find."

"I'll drink to that," said Prince Kellan, raising his tankard in salute. He took a deep swallow and sighed, smacking his lips. "I swear, I think you might be right."

Princess Lilliana picked up her tankard and took a delicate sip. She smiled. "I don't drink much beer, but this really is a most pleasant flavour."

Belasko raised his own tankard. "Your health, your majesty, and yours, your highnesses — and to your prosperity, Kander." He took a sip and smiled at the innkeeper. "Now my friend, what are we having for dinner?"

The innkeeper cleared his throat. "Kendra has prepared a meal that is, in her own words, simple and hearty." He flushed. "According to her there are only so many stuffed larks' tongues a man can take."

Prince Kellan hooted with laughter. "By God, she's bold but she's not wrong."

The rest of the meal passed in good humour. Belasko and the royal guests praised the quality of the food in such terms that set Kander's ears to blazing, and at last, replete, they nursed full stomachs and glasses of brandy.

King Mallor sighed. "I say, Belasko, you were not wrong. That was as fine a meal as I've had in quite some time."

Prince Kellan took a large swig of brandy. "The innkeeper's got a good cellar too. Damn fine beer, followed by damn fine wines, and now a damn fine brandy."

The king scowled at his son. "Of course that would be what you took from this evening."

Prince Kellan returned his father's scowl. "And what is that supposed to mean?"

King Mallor gestured expansively with his brandy glass. "The entire repast we've just enjoyed — delicious, flavourful, perfectly seasoned, and yes, with well-matched drinks. An evening spent in intelligent conversation with good company, venturing out into the city beyond our usual rounds. And the thing you fixate on is the alcohol."

The prince shrugged, a sullen expression working its way across his face. "So? A man is allowed a few vices."

King Mallor snorted. "A few vices? There's precious few you *don't* have. When I was your age..."

Oh dear, here we go.

"When you were my age you were already king, and wed," snapped Prince Kellan. "If you want me to act responsibly then maybe you should give me some responsibilities, instead of hoarding everything for yourself."

A loud bang reverberated around the room as the king slammed his hand down on the table. "Responsibilities? If you acted responsibly in the first place..." His face reddened and his voice grew louder as he spoke.

"Your majesty, your highness, please," Belasko interjected, "let us not spoil an enjoyable evening. There is a place and a time for such arguments. Far be it for me to proscribe you, but I think that now may not be such."

Glowering at each other, tempers still simmering beneath the surface, the king and prince both settled back into their chairs. Lilliana toyed with the stem of her wine glass, avoiding eye contact. King Mallor forced a smile. "You are right, of course. As you so often are." His expression softened. "I'm sorry, son. I am quick to anger, but have only your best interests at heart."

Prince Kellan gave his own hesitant smile, before leaning forward and placing his hand on his father's. "I know, Father. Apologies. I have created a part for myself and sometimes I feel forced to play it. As you say, the food was exceptional tonight. I propose we offer this girl the position."

Mallor nodded, squeezing his son's hand in response. "I agree. Lilliana, what do you think?"

Princess Lilliana, who had remained silent through the outburst, gave a sad smile. "I think that it's a shame our dinners must so often end in argument — but the food was exquisite. We should definitely have this talent in the palace kitchens."

King Mallor nodded. "Agreed on all points. Belasko, could you send one of the guards to fetch Kander and his daughter — what is her name? Kendra?"

Belasko stood, pushing back his chair. "Of course, your majesty." He went to the door, opened it and murmured a few words to one of the guards outside, before closing it again and returning to the table. He poured all of them another measure of the brandy from the decanter that Kander had thoughtfully left on the table, before retaking his seat. Belasko raised his glass to the light before taking a sip. "You know," he murmured, "your highness is correct. This is damn fine brandy."

The king snorted, the prince and princess laughed, and there came a tap at the door.

"Enter," said the king.

Kander came in with Kendra close behind. She was muttering to herself about the arrogance of patrons bidding them enter in their own inn, when she laid eyes on their evening's guests. Those eyes went wide as saucers and she dropped into a deep curtsy. "Your majesty, your highnesses. I had no idea... I hope our poor table hasn't offended you." She stood back up, glaring at her father. "I'd have offered better if I knew who was dining with us."

King Mallor laughed. "Peace young lady, don't blame your father. I asked him to keep our presence a secret, and your table was far from poor. I can't remember the last time I had a meal as satisfying. You know, there really *is* such a thing as too many stuffed larks' tongues." Kendra blushed, shooting her father another look. The king cleared his throat. "However, you will still have to learn how to prepare such delicacies when you start work in the palace kitchens."

Kendra flushed. "When I... Do you mean to say — that is, your majesty — are you offering me a job?"

Princess Lilliana smiled. "He most certainly is. If you'll take it?"

Kendra nodded vigorously. "Yes, of course your highness, I'd be honoured. Oh, thank you! Thank you so much."

"Belasko will arrange the details, as well as providing adequate compensation for the meal we've enjoyed tonight. What do you think, a gold sovereign?"

Both Kander and Kendra gawped. "Your majesty," said the innkeeper, "that's far too generous..."

"Nonsense." The king dismissed his objection with a wave of his hand. "I feel it is almost too little compensation for robbing you of such a fine cook. Now, if you wouldn't mind leaving us to finish our brandy, we won't take up too much more of your evening."

Once they'd shuffled out, offering effusive thanks, the four dining companions looked at each other.

"Well, Belasko," said the king, "that was well done."

"Thank you, your majesty. I know you like to see talent rewarded."

"Just as you hate to see it wasted. You were right, that young woman's skills deserve a chance to shine."

"Speaking of shining," Prince Kellan stood, draining his brandy glass. "I have a very bright possibility of an evening's entertainment to pursue. If you'll excuse me, Father?"

Mallor looked his son over before nodding his assent. "Thank you for coming with us, son. We should do things like this more often."

Kellan grinned at his father. "You won't find me arguing.

Good night Father, good night Sister. Good night Belasko." He tipped them all a salute, picked up his cloak, and left. Lilliana also stood.

"If you'll forgive me Father, I feel the need for some fresh air after that brandy. Would you mind if I joined the guards outside before we return to the palace?"

"Of course not my dear one, we'll be just behind you."

Princess Lilliana smiled before putting on her cloak and making her way out of the room

King Mallor sighed, shaking his head.

"What is it, your majesty?" Belasko asked.

"I fear for my children, and for our people. If anything were to happen to me... If neither of my children marry and produce an heir soon then the line of succession isn't clear. Distant cousins and foreign powers that we're tied to by blood might make claim to the throne. There could be civil war as our country descends into the sort of squabbling behaviour for which we used to look down on our southern neighbours. And with added pressure from that southern quarter..." He shook his head again. "There's still time for both of them, but that son of mine... As much as I love him, I can't help but think he's not showing any signs of being ready for kingship."

"It is true that he enjoys himself, but—"

"Enjoys himself?" The king snorted. "He spends his evenings, every evening, carousing with wastrels. Drinking and whoring, in and out of the worst parts of the city. Between the two of us, I'm concerned that if he doesn't temper his behaviour then before long we'll have a royal bastard to contend with, if he hasn't fathered one already. Now Lilliana is a much more sober child. Behaves in a way suited to her station."

"I won't disagree with you sire, not to either of your children's merits or misfortunes. However, I think Kellan would surprise you, given the chance."

Mallor raised an eyebrow. "You do, do you?" A look flashed

in his eyes, the message clear: *know your place*. King Mallor had done much to ease the stuffy formality of the court that he had inherited from his father, but even so Belasko's origins were not always easily overcome.

Belasko leaned forward in his chair. "I do. I think, if given more responsibility, he would show himself to be... Well, responsible. At heart he wants to please you, to impress. He only acts out in the way he does out of boredom, I'm sure of it. Give him something to do and I think he would rise to the challenge."

The king pursed his lips, thinking. Eventually he sighed. "You might be right, although I fear it may well be too late. I'm loathe to offer him something until he's proven himself."

"How can he ever prove himself ready, if he's never given the opportunity?"

Mallor laughed at that, draining his own glass and making to rise. "Well said. Maybe you don't keep your brain in your scabbard after all."

2

The palace kitchens were a hot and busy place, a bustling network of rooms dedicated to preparing, producing, and preserving food for the royal household. There were multiple pantries and larders, kitchens full of ovens for baking, fireplaces for roasting, cooking pots and cauldrons bubbling away, all combining to make a fragrant and noisy workplace. It teemed with staff in their uniforms of white aprons embroidered with the royal sigil, worn over sturdy work clothes. Amongst all that, Kendra's new colleagues still managed to make themselves heard.

"Where did you say you worked before?"

Kendra sighed. They all knew she had worked at an inn, that she was a 'discovery', that Belasko had helped arrange her new job. The only reason they kept asking was to try and hammer home a point. You do not belong. You shouldn't be here. You should go back to your inn and remember your place.

They were a group of the other kitchen staff who had decided that she wasn't worthy to work in their august company, some younger than her, some older, but all with the same chip on their shoulder. Some of them were gathered around her now, while she worked to prepare their midday meal.

"The same place as when you last asked, Tarvin."

Tarvin grinned. He was a lanky youth who had taken to picking on her. Other staff had gathered around, letting Tarvin do the talking while they sniggered up their sleeves. "Oh yes, your family inn, wasn't it? How was it you managed to get a job here again? It's quite a jump from an inn in one of the, um, *lesser* parts of town, to the palace kitchens."

Kendra sighed again, before using a long spoon to taste the stew she was preparing. She nodded to herself, satisfied. "You know the answer to that question, too. You ask it often enough." A few of the other staff laughed at that. Perhaps she was winning a few of them over. "You'll see what kind of cook I am in a few minutes, if you can stop talking long enough to put something in your mouth."

"Oh," Tarvin murmured under his breath, moving closer, "I'm sure I can stop talking long enough for something..."

The other staff had gone silent, uncomfortable at the turn that events had taken. Tarvin reached out a hand to grab hold of her but stopped short, a look of surprise on his face.

Kendra laughed. "That's right, look down why don't you?" Tarvin did as she bid, wincing at the extremely sharp kitchen knife she held to his crotch, catching at the material of his apron and pressing into the clothes and flesh beneath. "Did I tell you my father was a soldier? He taught me to look after myself. Remember that the next time you try to lay hands on me, or you might end up missing some essential equipment."

Tarvin had gone white as a sheet. Trembling, he backed away. From a safe distance he gathered himself, then spat at her feet. "That's for you, whore. As if I would even want to touch you." With that he stalked off, alone. His acolytes decided not to follow and dispersed to their own places in the kitchens.

How long will it be like this? Kendra thought to herself. *Two weeks now, and still the other staff don't warm to me. I didn't think it would be like this.*

Later that day Belasko came to visit her. She was preparing a dessert, when a voice at her elbow surprised her.

"Settling in okay?"

She whirled around, clutching a wooden spoon. When she saw who it was she relaxed and smiled. "Oh Belasko, sorry, you made me jump. Yes, well enough, thank you. I'm actually cooking for the royal table now."

The king's champion nodded, looking around the room. "Everyone treating you alright?"

"Mostly, yes."

"Mostly? Some haven't? Let me guess: that lanky string of piss is one of them?" He nodded towards the far corner, where Tarvin was taking a tray of cakes out of one of the big ovens. He had been glaring at them but, surprised at being noticed, he became very interested in his work.

Kendra laughed. "Yes. A few of them have been unpleasant, Tarvin there chief among them. They seem to think they're above a cook from a humble inn."

Belasko snorted. "Some people born into below-stairs families seem to think they have the standing of their above-stairs masters. Ridiculous. We're all working people. Why should it matter where you're from? It should be about what you can do."

He was frowning now. She studied him for a moment, taking in the broad shoulders that tapered to a narrow waist, the averagely handsome face. He wasn't overly tall, but carried himself well. He walked into any room like he was taking command of it, and there was a steady confidence to him that she liked. Belasko was dressed for travelling, a woollen cloak over a black, fitted jacket chased with silver embroidery, white shirt peeking through at the collar. He wore sturdy breeches over his stockings and knee-high riding boots. Blushing, she realised that her moment of observation had stretched a little long. "It's alright. Pellero, the head chef, has taken a liking to me — or rather, to my food."

Belasko laughed. "Oh, that old rogue. Yes, he'll like you well enough as long as you keep him fed. What are you making there?"

She gestured to her workstation. "Poached pears, the same as I made when you brought the king and prince to our inn. They seem to have become the prince's favourite dessert, he wants them every evening. I'm making them just for him tonight — everyone else is having something different."

"Good, I'm glad. Unfortunately I won't get to see him enjoy them. I was due to dine at the royal table, but I've been called away to the Academy on business. I'll be back soon, in a few days. Let me know if you have any more trouble with the other staff. I can't stand bullies."

"I will, thank you. And thank you for coming by as well, I owe you for helping get me this position. I won't forget it."

He smiled. "That's quite alright. I like to see talent rewarded. I'll see you again soon." Belasko left, exchanging a few words with some of the other staff on his way out. He waved to Pellero, who was observing the kitchen from a stool in the centre of the room, before ducking out the door.

A short while later there was another visitor to the kitchen, a man dressed in the black of the inquisition. The presence of one of the king's own investigators, those tasked with rooting out threats to the crown, could dampen any atmosphere. The general hubbub of the kitchen subsided as he knocked at the door and waited until one of the staff could attend to him.

Pellero himself lumbered over and a few words were exchanged before the head chef nodded and pointed Kendra out. The inquisitor looked over and she met his eyes — or rather, eye. With a start she realised he had only one, his left eye covered with a black patch. The inquisitor nodded at her, then beckoned her over with a crooked finger. Kendra swallowed around a lump that felt lodged in her throat.

"Hey," she called to Allana, the cook working nearest to her. "Can you keep an eye on this please? Make sure it doesn't boil over?" Allana's eyes flicked up from her own work to meet Kendra's gaze only briefly. She nodded, otherwise expressionless. "Thank you!" Kendra said, before leaving her work station and making her way over to the door.

She curtsied when she got close to the inquisitor. "Hello sir, how can I help?" she said as she straightened.

He looked down at her, a tall man with a shock of sandy hair, face unreadable. He may have been clad in the black of the Inquisition, but the fine detailing and tailoring on his jacket marked him out as a man of rank as much as did the golden sun and twin stars picked out on his shoulder. Clearly a man that took pride in his appearance, he was immaculately turned out. The collar and cuffs of his shirt neatly pressed into crisp lines, boots polished until they shone, golden jacket buttons gleaming. He attempted a smile but it didn't seem like an expression with which his face was familiar. "Just a few questions Miss, routine when someone starts in a position close to the royal family. It should have been attended to before. My apologies for disrupting your work."

She returned his unsure smile with a warmer one of her own. "That's alright sir, ask me anything you like."

"Thank you." He took out a small sheaf of papers and a charcoal pencil from a pouch at his belt. "First of all, your name?"

"Kendra, sir."

He nodded, jotting as he went. “And were you born here in the city?”

“Yes, sir.”

“Father’s name and occupation?”

“Kander sir, an innkeeper.”

“An inn in the city?”

“Yes sir, the Golden Hind, over by the fourth gate.”

The inquisitor nodded. “I know it. Not the best part of town, but the inn has a good reputation. Your mother?

“Dead, sir.”

He grimaced. “My condolences.”

“That’s alright, it’s been a long time.”

The inquisitor nodded. “Well, an old grief can still sting. Are you married?”

“I was, sir. My husband died in the sweating sickness that came through our neighbourhood a few years back. It’s just me and my boy now.”

“I’m sorry, a lot of people lost family in that illness. You say you have a son; how old is he?”

“Five years. My father cares for him while I’m working in the kitchens, with some help. He’s a sweet-natured boy, but always falling into mischief. ”

The inquisitor gave a more genuine smile this time. “That is, I understand, the nature of small children.” He tucked away his sheaf of papers and pencil and gave her a nod. “That’s all I need. Again, I’m sorry to disturb. What is it I’ve taken you away from?”

“I’m making poached pears for the prince’s dessert. They seem to have become his favourite.”

“Well then, far be it for me to keep our good prince from his dessert. Good evening, Mistress Kendra.”

“And to you, sir.”

The inquisitor gave her a shallow bow, then turned and was on his way.

Kendra went to go back to her work and frowned. Tarvin was walking away from her work station. What was he doing there? She walked back, looking over her things and inspecting the pears, but nothing seemed to be amiss. Kendra looked over at Allana, who had been keeping an eye on her station but she was absorbed in her own work. She looked over at Tarvin but he avoided her gaze, keeping his attention on what he was doing. She inspected the dessert she had been working on. Taking a very small spoonful of the sauce and a slim sliver of flesh from one of the pears, Kendra raised them to her nose. She sniffed them and, having detected nothing out of the ordinary, tentatively tasted. Both seemed fine. Kendra shrugged. Whatever mischief was on the boy's mind, he clearly hadn't managed to carry it out.

The rest of the meal preparation passed quietly, for the most part. A member of the Baskan ambassador's staff appeared as they were putting the finishing touches on the evening meal. He gave Pellero strict instructions regarding a traditional Baskan dish that was due to be served at a reception in a few days' time. A small, thin, balding man with a stony face, he insisted on a tour of the kitchens. Remarking all the while on the differences between the kitchen at the royal palace in the Baskan capital, not all of them favourable, he then left.

It was later that evening, as she cleaned down her countertop, that Kendra became aware of a commotion from the service end of the kitchen. There were screams and shouting, and then three guardsmen burst through the service doors into the kitchen.

"No one leave!" shouted the first guard, a grim look on his face. "The prince is dead. Murdered. No one is allowed to leave."

Kendra looked around her, taking in a view that had not changed for the last few hours. She was terrified, her surroundings giving her nothing to do but contemplate her fate. To make matters worse she had been violently ill, several times, and was now shivering uncontrollably. She and the rest of the kitchen staff had been escorted down to the palace dungeons, in the basement of one of the palace's far-flung towers. They had been separated and placed into solitary cells, presumably so they couldn't confer over the shocking events of the day.

Prince Kellan dead, Kendra thought to herself. *I can't believe it. I know some thought ill of him, but he seemed so nice.*

Her cell was small, the ceiling only just high enough for her to stand up. A rough pallet along one wall and a filthy bucket were her only comforts. A small grate up near the ceiling would presumably let in some light during the day, though it was fully dark now. As summer was now ended and the longer nights of autumn were drawing in, this grate would let in less and less light over time. One wall was made entirely of bars, granting her no privacy from outside observers. A portion of this wall was a locked gate that swung inward when opened. Hers was just one in a line of cells along the corridor, the furthest from the entrance, although none of the other cells seemed to be occupied. The atmosphere was damp and cold, smelling of mould, her own vomit, and more unpleasant things.

I wonder what time it is? It must be hours since dinner service.

The only light came from some crude torches in wall sconces along the corridor. They emitted an unpleasant black smoke and the light they cast was faltering and sickly, matching Kendra's feelings perfectly.

There came an echo of footsteps from down the corridor, drawing nearer. Kendra tried to stand up straight, chin up, determined to meet whoever came as boldly as she could. But she found herself swaying slightly, shivering with whatever ague had hold of her. The footsteps slowed as they approached, until a figure appeared in front of her cell. It was the one-eyed inquisitor she had spoken to earlier that day. He slowed to a stop outside her cell, regarding her in silence for a long moment. When he cleared his throat it made her jump.

"Mistress Kendra. I didn't expect to see you again so soon."

"Nor I you, sir."

"No. I'm sure you would have no reason to expect to see me again. None at all." He reached into a shadowed alcove in the wall behind him, pulling out a short three-legged stool on which he sat in silence, looking at her.

Kendra broke the silence first. "Sir, is it true? What the guards said? Is the prince... dead?"

He nodded slowly. "I'm afraid so. It is a dark day."

"Oh, Aronos, lord of all, preserve him, the poor man." Kendra found that her hands were shaking and clutched them together. "A dark day indeed. Evil, even."

The inquisitor had noticed her hands. "Ah dear Kendra, is it too cold in here for you? Or is it something else? Are you scared?"

"Of course I'm scared," Kendra blurted. "The prince is dead and all of the kitchen staff have been dragged off into cells. It's cold in here, I feel sick, and I'm worried for my son. They will have expected me home hours ago."

He nodded slowly, deliberately. "Well, it seems like the prince was poisoned. Something slipped into his dinner. Surely you can see we had to round up the kitchen staff?"

"Poisoned? Oh, dear god..."

"I'm afraid so. As to the condition of your accommodation, well..." The inquisitor waved his hands vaguely to indicate her cell. "Where else would you put people you needed to question? Now, your family. I will send a note to your father at the Golden Hind to let him know that you're helping us with our enquiries. Alright?"

Kendra nodded, smiling weakly. “Thank you sir, that is most kind.”

He waved away her thanks. “Not at all, it’s the least I can do. After all, I’m sure you’re going to be very helpful, aren’t you?”

“Yes sir, I’ll do all that I can to help.”

“Good, good. That’s... good.” The inquisitor relaxed on his stool, leaning back to rest against the wall. He crossed one leg over the other, idly tapping on one of his boots with a fingernail. “I’m sure you can be helpful to us. It’s to do with the food the prince ate this evening. We’re trying to narrow down the source of his poisoning and we’ve discovered that this evening the prince ate exactly the same food as everyone else. Except for one thing.” He paused, watching her expectantly. There was silence, apart from the tap-tap-tap of his fingernail on his boot.

Eventually Kendra spoke. “It was the pears, wasn’t it? The ones I prepared. They were the only thing the prince had that was different to everyone else.”

The inquisitor leaned forwards. “Yes, that’s right. I believe you prepared them for him specially?”

Belasko was nearly ready to set off on the journey to the Academy, which was housed on his land outside the city, when a detachment of the palace guards rode into the courtyard of his city house, horseshoes ringing off the flagstones. They wore the black and gold of the royal house, a silver stag embroidered on their surcoats, and pulled up with a clatter of armour, surrounding him and his travelling companions. There was quite a crowd in the courtyard already, Belasko’s staff having just finished the preparations for departure and loading up the pack horses. Orren, his long-time companion and manager of the Academy, put one hand to the blade at his waist. The air was thick with tension.

Belasko held up a hand. "Peace, friends! We'll find no trouble from the palace guard, I'm sure. Still your hands. We don't want anyone getting excited."

Orren gave him a flat look before reluctantly taking his hand from his sword hilt. Belasko had yet to mount, so led his horse by the reins, walking up to the woman who seemed to be leading the troops.

"Hello there. Do you command these guards? Hang on — is that Majel? Difficult to see in this light." It was getting darker, although sunset was still a while off and the lanterns were unlit in the courtyard.

A sharp-featured young woman with a fierce expression and her dark hair cut short, the rider sat up straight in her saddle. "It is, sir. And yes, I command these troops."

"Good to see you, it's been a while. Still practising those drills I gave you?" Belasko reached up and clasped the young commander's hand, giving it a firm shake.

"That I am sir, and I think I've seen some improvement. It's good to see you too, although I wish the circumstances were different."

Belasko leaned back, taking in the tension the riders showed for the first time. "Why, what are the circumstances?"

Majel swallowed. "I'm sorry to say we've been sent to escort you back to the palace. You're needed there."

Belasko nodded. "Of course, that's no problem. Are my people free to return to the Academy? They're due back this evening and their families will worry otherwise."

"My orders are only for you, sir. They are free to carry on their way."

"Thank you, Majel." Belasko spoke to his people. "Alright, you carry on home. Orren, remember what we said about the east pasture. I think we need to put in some sort of drainage there. Can you look into it and we'll make a decision when I'm back?"

Orren nodded, his shaggy blonde hair swaying. "Alright. Make sure you come back when you can. There's decisions need making before winter that are above my station."

Belasko laughed. "Nonsense, you run the place so well I swear I'm hardly needed. Off you go now, I'll be safe in Majel's hands. Fare thee well."

Orren nodded again, raising a hand in salute to his friend and master, then to the young commander, and set heels to his horse's flanks. The others that rode with him clattered off behind, calling out their own farewells. As they disappeared through the gates, Belasko mounted his own horse and turned to Majel. "Shall we?" They set off down the wide cobbled road, the troops falling in behind as Belasko's household staff closed the courtyard gates.

Belasko looked at the young commander. "How long has it been now since you were at the Academy. Four years?"

Majel smiled. "Five, sir."

Belasko nodded. "Is it really? You seem to be doing well for yourself. You were a good student, you know."

"I had a good teacher."

They rode on in silence for several minutes.

"Majel," Belasko said, "what's really going on? Why am I needed at the palace?"

Majel looked down, muttering something under her breath. Belasko leaned closer to her. "What was that? I couldn't quite catch it." He was surprised to see tears in the eyes of his former student when she looked back up.

"Damn it," Majel said. "They didn't want me to tell you. But how can I not?"

"Tell me what?"

Majel cleared her throat, looking away when she spoke. "It's Prince Kellan. He's... he's dead."

Belasko felt the bottom of his stomach drop away, as if a pit had just opened up inside him. "No," he whispered, "that can't be."

Majel turned back to him, angry now as much as upset. "It shouldn't be, but it can and it is."

"What happened? Some kind of accident? I saw him myself only earlier today."

"Poison." Majel spat the word, face wrinkling in disgust.

"How? The palace is the most secure building in Villan. How could he be poisoned?"

Majel shook her head. "I don't know. But that is what the inquisition are going to find out."

Kendra stared at the inquisitor in shock. "That's... that's impossible. I prepared the pears myself. No one else went near them."

The inquisitor met her gaze. "Well, that's a problem then, isn't it? Are you saying that you poisoned the prince?"

Kendra felt the blood drain from her face. "Me? No, I-I wouldn't, I didn't, I couldn't do that!"

He nodded. "I'm sure. Where would a humble cook procure poison in the first place? Particularly one that must have been expensive, being undetectable in the food either by taste or scent. A rare poison indeed, requiring deeper pockets than you possess. Are you sure that no one else went near the dish during preparation?"

Kendra's mind raced. "I can't think of anyone — wait! After we had our conversation earlier today I saw Tarvin, one of the other kitchen staff, walking away from my station. Allana was watching my station, but could he have slipped something into the food?"

The inquisitor shrugged. "I don't think so, I had my eye on him while we talked." He smiled, tapping his eye patch with his forefinger. "Forgive my attempt at humour. I was watching him and didn't see him interfere with the food you were preparing. I have already spoken to Tarvin and he confessed that he intended to spoil it, as a prank, but was put off by my presence and didn't carry it out. Are you sure there was no one else? No other visitors today? Anything out of the ordinary?"

Kendra put her head in her hands, thinking, desperate to find a clue that would help prove her own innocence. She looked up.

"We had a visit from one of the Baskan ambassador's staff, bringing Pellero instructions for a Baskan dish that was due to be served at a reception this week."

Ervan raised his eyebrows. "Really? Now that is interesting. Do you remember if they passed by your work station at all?"

Kendra frowned, then shook her head. "No. He toured the kitchen but I don't remember him coming close to where I was working."

"Hmm... Can you describe him for me?"

"Middle aged, thin, balding. Face like a stone."

Ervan nodded. "Thank you. I'll add it to my notes and see if someone can pay the ambassadorial residence a visit. Now, were there any other visitors today? Anyone that came to your station, could have interfered with your work."

Something occurred to Kendra then: a thought, albeit an unpleasant one. She swallowed before she spoke. "There was one other. One other visitor today."

The inquisitor arched an eyebrow. "Oh? Who was that?"

Kendra shook her head. "But I'm sure it couldn't be, it's not possible..."

"I'll decide what's possible. You just tell me who came to visit you."

Kendra struggled to get the words out, tears coming. "Belasko. He-he came to visit me. To-to see how I was getting on."

"I see. Was the dish you were preparing left unattended at any point when he was with you, or were you distracted at all?"

"No, not left unattended. But-but I did look away once or twice, just for a moment. I'm sure it wasn't possible for him to — I mean, I just looked away for the briefest moment..." Her shoulders were shaking as she sobbed.

"There, there. I know it's upsetting. It's been an upsetting day for us all." He leaned forwards on his stool. "You think it was too short a time for him to have slipped something into the food, but I've seen Belasko fight." He tapped his eye patch again. "Before I lost this, when my vision was good. I know what his reflexes are like. The man can move quicker than a striking snake when he needs to. If anyone could have done it in a moment's distraction, it is Belasko."

Kendra tried to bring her sobs under control. "But he's loyal to the king, and the prince was his friend. Everyone knows that. Why would he do something like that?"

"That," said the inquisitor, "is for me to find out. We've sent men after Belasko, to bring him back to the palace."

"You've already sent men for him? But I only just told you that he came to the kitchens."

"Oh, I already knew that. I just wanted to see if you would tell me." The inquisitor stood, replacing his stool in the alcove. "Now, you said you've been sick. How are you feeling now? Achy, nauseas, shivery?" Kendra nodded. "Did you taste any of the dessert you were making?"

Again, Kendra nodded. "After I saw Tarvin near my station, I tasted a little of the sauce. A small slice of pear. I couldn't see or smell anything wrong with the dish, I just wanted to make sure he hadn't tampered with it." Another bout of shivering struck her.

Ervan sighed. "Then you have taken a small dose of the poison that killed the prince. I will arrange a draught from the royal physician that should help." He smiled at her, the expression not reaching his eye. "You really have been most helpful. I'll see to that note for your family, and someone to fetch you some blankets and a brazier. You might be here a while." He turned and walked away, and Kendra was left alone with only the flickering torchlight and the echo of his footsteps for company.

~

The cell door slammed shut behind Belasko. *I should have known something was off when they asked for my sword at the gate. 'Precautions' my arse.*

It had been an embarrassing moment, for him and the guards. Majel had held her hand out, not meeting his eyes. "I'm sorry sir, I have my orders. None but the palace guard are to go armed within the walls until further notice."

Belasko had paused, reluctant to hand over his sword. He had not gone without a weapon in a long time. "I understand, although asking the king's champion to go unarmed when it is the royal family that has been harmed seems a little foolish to me."

Majel sighed. "To me too, but still..."

"Orders are orders. I understand. Here." He unbuckled his sword belt and handed it and his rapier to the young commander. "Look after this for me. At least then I know it's in good hands."

Majel swallowed as she took the weight of Belasko's blade. "Of course, sir. It'll be a privilege. Belasko. I, um, I need to escort you in now."

"Of course. Where are we going? To the royal chambers? I would like to see the king and whoever is leading the investigation."

"Well, the latter won't be a problem. They've asked to see you right away. I'm to take you now, to wait for them."

"Where are we going?"

Majel looked ashamed as she spoke. "To the dungeons, sir. They want to speak to you there."

"The dungeons. Majel? What's going on?"

"I don't know, sir. I'm sure it's all some mistake. Just come with me. The sooner they talk to you, the sooner this will all be sorted out."

Belasko let his former student lead him to the dungeons and place him in a cell, an uneasy feeling building as he went. Little did he know it, but his cell was the twin of Kendra's, right down to the damp and mouldy air. He turned as the door closed behind him.

"Shouldn't I be in chains? The imagery would certainly suit the venue, don't you think?"

Majel shifted from one foot to the other, shamefaced. *Poor woman. It's not her fault.* "Sorry, I know you are only doing your duty. Go tell whoever it is that wants to see me that I'm here and we can get this farce over with."

Majel nodded, turned and left. Hours passed and Belasko waited. And waited. There was no sign of anyone coming to question him. Finally his impatience got the better of him and he started to call out.

"Come on! I've been waiting for hours. Is there anyone there? This is ridiculous!" He called and shouted, banging on the bars of his cell, rattling the door in its hinges.

Eventually he heard footsteps approaching. He quieted himself, waiting to see who would appear. A figure emerged out of the gloom, dressed head-to-toe in black. *The Inquisition, then. That makes sense,* Belasko thought to himself, although he still felt a shiver run through him at the thought of being at the mercies of a member of that institution. Originally a semi-religious order created to bend people's worship to Aronos, the Sun God, and away from their old pagan ways, one of the king's ancestors had turned them into a not-so-secret police force.

They had a terrifying reputation and it was considered best to avoid their notice. As they drew closer the figure's face became clear: a man with a shock of sandy hair, one eye covered by a patch. *The face is familiar...*

The inquisitor stopped outside his cell, looking him up and down. "Sorry," he said at last. "Busy night."

"I'm sure," said Belasko, "but what am I doing in the cells? Let me help you. I'm sure I can assist the investigation. I need to see the king, the poor man. Is the palace locked down, no one in or out since..." Belasko stopped, unable to say the words.

"Since the prince was poisoned at his own table? Yes, we do know what we're doing, thank you. As for seeing the king, I'm afraid that's impossible. He's quite distraught, as I'm sure you understand."

"Yes, of course. I just wish to bring what comfort I can."

"That would be precious little, being the source of at least some of his present misery."

Belasko blinked. "What? How?"

The inquisitor sighed. "Not only has his son just been murdered, but to find out that he has been betrayed by someone who was trusted above all others..."

Belasko felt suddenly cold all over, as if he had been pushed into an icy lake. He struggled to get his breath. "What... what are you saying?"

The inquisitor smirked. "Just that a rather incriminating letter was found in the king's apartments this evening. That and other evidence gathered tonight means that you, Belasko, king's champion, are the foremost suspect in the murder of our prince."

Belasko could only stare at the man in black, who shrugged again. "I'm sure you will protest your innocence, but the evidence is rather stacking up against you. You'll have a chance to answer my questions tomorrow. Try to get some rest, if you can. It's been a long day."

"No," Belasko said as the inquisitor turned and walked away. "It's not true. It's not possible. The king can't believe that. He knows me too well, knows I love him and Kellan both. He must know I would never..." He was at the bars to his cell now, shouting between them at the retreating back of the inquisitor. "I would never hurt the prince. I'm innocent! Please, send for the king. I must see the king!"

The inquisitor, unmoved, faded into implacable shadow as Belasko slumped against the bars of his cell.

It can't be. It just can't be.

3

Dawn brought with it a bowl of unappetising gruel, and his first visitor. *This food would be enough to break a man's spirit in time, never mind the accommodation.* He stirred the grey slop with a spoon. A wooden spoon, to match the wooden bowl the gruel was served in. *Of course, you wouldn't want to give a prisoner anything they could use to harm themselves — or use as a weapon.* He chuckled. *Belasko, most deadly with a bowl and spoon!*

The sound of footsteps brought him out of his reverie. Setting the bowl down, he stood, moving to the bars of his cell to see who would come. Surprise was followed by a wave of relief that washed over him when he saw it was Orren. His friend reached between the bars to clasp his hand, and for a moment they regarded each other in silence. A silence Orren broke.

The big man shook his head. "This is a fine mess we've got to unpick, isn't it?"

Belasko threw his hands up in the air. "Don't I know it? You know of course, that I'm not guilty?"

Orren snorted. "Well, obviously. You loved the prince like a brother. There's no way you'd have been part of an assassination attempt. The number of times you've saved his life, or dragged him out of bar fights and bad situations of his own making. No one who knows you would think you're guilty. No one with half a brain, anyway."

"That's what I thought. So why are the Inquisition holding me here? If they have evidence then they should bring it to me and let me respond. This is maddening."

Orren shrugged. "Which is probably the point."

Belasko drummed his fingers on one of the cell bars. "I swear I recognised the inquisitor who visited me last night."

"Visited you? Are you alright?" His friend peered through the bars, looking him over for any sign of injury. "A visit from the Inquisition usually means one thing."

"I'm fine. He just dropped by to let me know I'm apparently the main suspect and that he'll be by again today to ask me some questions."

"He probably wanted to let you stew on that for a while." Orren scratched his chin. "I'll tell you, I had a devil of a time getting in to see you."

Belasko arched an eyebrow. "How did you manage it? I thought the palace was on lockdown and you had left the city."

Orren laughed. "You didn't think we'd go far, did you? Majel marching you up to the palace looked enough like an arrest to make me nervous. Plenty of the palace guard owe me favours or money at dice. I just had to wait until one came on duty that I could guilt into letting me in. Eventually, Darin — you remember her? An older woman, served in the Last War — she came on duty. Then it was easy."

"Darin, I do remember her. A good soldier by all accounts, although we never served together."

"I'll tell you Belasko, you've most of the palace guard on your side. You've trained enough of them, and the rest, well, they know you to be a good man. A loyal man. They know you'd never have done this. Also, poison? Not your style."

"That's good to know. I hope the king feels the same way."

Orren frowned. "Has he not been to see you?"

Belasko shook his head. "No. I have asked to speak with him, and I will keep on asking. If I could just talk to him, I know I could make him realise how ridiculous this is. I should be helping with the investigation, not be the focus of it."

"He knows you well enough. I expect he'll come to his senses when things calm down. Listen, I have to go — I shouldn't be down here, Darin will only look the other way for so long. But I'll keep pestering on your behalf. Is there anything you need?"

Belasko sighed, picking up the bowl of gruel from the floor. "A more appetising breakfast?"

Orren reached through the bars to once again clasp his hand. "Good. Keep that sense of humour. I'll be back when I can." They shook hands, then Belasko was left once again alone.

Orren's visit made Belasko think back through the long days of his and Orren's friendship. Orren and he, terrified before their first battle, exultant after it, having faced death and lived to tell the tale. Teasing each other about flings that they had while on leave, until one day Orren, eyes shining, could not stop talking about the most beautiful girl he had ever seen. Denna. And Belasko's heart had broken in his chest.

He remembered the day of their wedding, and how happy the two of them had been. Belasko had stood with Orren that day as, beaming with joy, the big man stumbled over the wedding recitations. Whooping and sweeping his new wife into an embrace when the first rays of the new day's sun had lit upon their hands, bound by leather cord, and the priest announced that as the day began, so did their life together.

All of these memories and more were running through his mind when he heard the clank of the door at the end of the corridor opening and closing, followed by the echoing click of footsteps. Belasko stood, waiting to see who would appear in front of his cell.

A woman in the blue and scarlet military uniform came out of the gloom, buttons and epaulets gleaming, medals shining on her chest. The thing that surprised Belasko most was that it was a Baskan uniform, and the woman wearing it was Aveyard, the Baskan ambassador.

A tall woman of middle years with chestnut hair and olive skin, she possessed a genial air, nothing seemed to faze her. Nor did she give anything away. The depths of her eyes hid who knew how many secrets, but the smile she turned on Belasko seemed at least to be genuine.

"There are some among my people who have longed to see this sight. Belasko, the villain of Dellan Pass, wrecker of our people's great dream, in chains. In a dungeon. Never would I have thought it would be *this* dungeon, your own king that had you placed in chains. I had to come and see it for myself, confirm what I had heard. I'm going to enjoy reporting this back to my superiors."

"Villain? My people remember that day very differently. And as you can see, I'm not wearing chains." Belasko held his wrists up to demonstrate.

"It's only a matter of time. Once you enter a dungeon..."

Belasko smiled. "I wouldn't know, I've never been in one before."

"Really? Not in all your adventures?" Aveyard sighed. "There's a first time for everything. Still, I have to thank you. Ordinarily if anything suspicious had happened to a member of the royal family, I'd expect to be the one answering questions, ambassadorial rank or not. Such is the tension still between our two peoples. As you've so handily incriminated yourself, I'm free to carry on about my business."

"I didn't do it," said Belasko quietly. "I didn't kill Kellan."

Aveyard laughed. "Of course not, my dear, but whoever *has* done it really wanted you to take the blame." Her face settled into a more serious expression. "There are some who would still suspect me of doing this, just to get my revenge on you for the disgrace you visited on my uncle."

Belasko shook his head. "There was no disgrace, just bad luck on his part and good luck on mine. He acquitted himself honourably. I rather liked him, actually, although we only met the once."

"He said the same of you. His life has never been the same since Dellan Pass. After you defeated his great gamble. It would be easy to blame you for that. To seek vengeance." Her expression was unreadable now, but her eyes bore into him.

Belasko met her gaze head-on. "There is something to honour among combatants. Your uncle said that to me during the war, and the apple would have fallen very far from the tree if you believed differently. I don't know you well, Ambassador, but I've never heard that you were one to take the easy path. If you agree that I'm innocent then why not help me prove it? Help me plead my case to the king?"

Aveyard laughed again, bitter this time. "Oh Belasko, you really are taken with yourself. I might not think you did it, I might not be the one who has set you up, but help you? No, no, no, my dear. I don't think so." She turned to walk away, calling over her shoulder as she left. "Good luck swordsman, you're going to need it."

"I've always had it before," he called after her. "Remember me to your uncle. He knows all about my luck."

Belasko's thoughts turned to the events of Dellan Pass, spurred by Ambassador Aveyard's's visit. What happened there had made Belasko's name and ensured his life would never be the same again.

It was supposed to be a simple scouting mission. He and Orren, inseparable since they had first been paired together in their initial training, were sent to scout Dellan Pass. The powers that be in the Villanese military had heard that Baskan forces were on the march and were determined to find out where. The infamous pass was so narrow that it was deemed impassable by any sizeable number of troops. Their generals were certain that the Baskans were taking a different route through the mountains, but wanted to make sure no smaller forces or scouts were going to make use of it. And so Belasko and Orren were sent to investigate. Both were young but had shown themselves capable, and were disappointed to have landed what felt like a pointless task.

"I'm telling you," Orren said as they rode into the rocky valley, "there's no way the Baskans are sending any troops through here, not even scouts. You have to go down to single file at the narrowest point."

"You're almost certainly not wrong, my friend," Belasko said over his shoulder as he led. "But we have our orders. The sooner we confirm there's no movements here, the sooner we can re-join our fellows."

Sheer grey cliffs rose raggedly up to either side, dotted with the scrubby brush and low-lying weeds that were the only signs of plant life. Their horses had to pick their way carefully over the broken rock of the valley floor. They were high up in the mountains that separated the nations of Villan and Bas and the air was thin and cold. Belasko looked around, taking in their desolate surroundings, and sighed.

"What is it?" asked Orren.

"Nothing. Just thinking that we get sent to all the best

places." Belasko grinned at his friend. "Join the army, they said. You'll be a hero, they said, impressing all the boys in your fancy uniform. It'll be a quick war, they said."

Orren laughed. "Aye, they said all that. Would you have joined if they'd told you the truth? That you'd spend most of your time bored, cold, hungry, or some combination of the three, dragging yourself through the arse end of nowhere?"

Belasko shook his head, a mock-rueful expression on his face. "They've a lot to answer for, those recruiters, truly."

It was some time later that they reached the narrowest point, where the cliffs almost came together, twisting around and back on themselves to form a switchback that made it impossible to see what was ahead. They both dismounted, tying up their horses to a thorny bush, before continuing on foot. Behind them their horses attempted to nibble at the bush, before giving up and moving on to a fruitless examination of the rocky ground, ever hopeful of something to eat.

"Quietly," Belasko said, "just in case there actually are any Baskans on the other side." Orren shook his head at this, but remained quiet.

They inched their way forwards, minding their step on the slippery rock, worn smooth by the passage of time. They had to go in single file, Belasko at the front, as they reached the switch-back. They rounded the corner and the pass began to open up again. Belasko stopped as the narrow passage turned back on itself once more and widened out into a larger valley. "Oh shit!"

The valley was full of Baskan infantry, as far as the eye could see.

Belasko and Orren backed themselves into the passage and began a whispered consultation.

"Aronos's great golden balls, what are they doing? Only a madman would bring an army through here," Orren hissed.

"Well then, the leaders of the Baskan army are clearly mad. Or they're trying to get the drop on us by doing something no one would ever expect, because it's mad. What are we going to do?"

Orren shrugged. "We were sent to scout — we've scouted, and found the devil's own load of the enemy. I say we get back to our own lines as fast as we can and tell them we've got visitors coming."

Belasko shook his head. "I didn't see much in the way of supplies, did you? I wager that they'll be moving at first light tomorrow. In which case they'd be onto Villanese soil before you could return with any force in numbers. Our nearest garrison is, what? A day's ride away? Half a day if you pushed your horse dangerously hard." He thought for a moment. "You go, you're the better rider. Take my horse as well so you can swap and rest one every few hours.

"If I go, what are you going to do?"

"I'll hold them here."

Orren stared at him, disbelief writ large across his face. He made a sound somewhere between a laugh, a cough, and a snort. "You'll hold them here? Half the Baskan army and you'll hold them here, on your own?"

Belasko looked back at his friend. "I know, it's madness. But if I go back to the narrowest point of the pass, it's single file. They'll have to come at me one at a time. I'll hold them as long as I can while you ride for help."

Orren grabbed him by the shoulders. "Damn right it's madness. Hell if I'm leaving you here on your own."

Belasko put his hand over one of Orren's. "That's just what you'll do. You're the better horseman, I'm the better swordsman. It's the only solution that doesn't leave us riding out of here with an army on our heels." His friend continued to stare at him, disbelieving. Belasko sighed. "Look, I don't like it either, but it's the only way. They look like they're dug in for the night, so they most likely won't move further into the pass until dawn tomorrow. It's early evening now. If you turn and ride for that garrison you can be there and back with mounted troops by this time tomorrow. If I can't hold them here I can at least make it difficult going for them, slow them down. With the rest of the army following behind, you'll be able to stop them moving far into Villanese territory, or bottle them up at the other end of the pass. Come on. It makes sense, and we don't have time to argue."

Orren sighed, before glaring at Belasko. "Alright, but I don't have to like it."

Some hours later, after Orren had departed, Belasko stood on his own watching the lights of the enemy camp. He had settled down on a rock, chewing a bit of dried beef from his rations. *No campfire for me tonight.* He swallowed, before biting off a bit more of the beef. *No sleep, either. I can't let them sneak up on me while I rest.* He snorted, aware of how ridiculous his situation was. *May all speed be with you, Orren. Come back soon. And bring some of our comrades-in-arms with you.*

Belasko's reverie was interrupted and his mind brought back to his present troubles as Viktor and Edred, two of the more annoying court functionaries, came to visit Belasko in his cell. The finery of their dress seemed at odds with the grim surroundings of the dungeon.

Belasko stood to greet them and was met with looks of disdain that bordered on open hostility. "Gentlemen," Belasko said, "I wish I was seeing you under better circumstances. I'd offer you some hospitality but, well," he gestured at their surroundings, "I have little to spare."

Viktor, ageing steward to the king, snorted. "I don't know how you can joke at a time like this." His face, which always looked like he had just tasted something sour, contorted even more than normal and his thinning silvery hair swayed as he shook his head.

Edred, his second, spat on the floor. "With the prince dead, and by your hand." Although younger than Viktor, he was still past his middle years. A fat man with curly black hair cut close to his head, his large belly strained at his doublet as if it wanted to burst free.

Belasko shook his head. "Not so. I loved the prince like a brother, you both know this to be true. I would never harm him. I should be out there helping catch his killer, not locked up in a cell."

"'Like a brother'?" Viktor sneered. "Just like you to think yourself brother to a prince. Don't forget where you came from, farmer's boy."

"How can I forget, when men like you so enjoy throwing it in my face?" Belasko eyed them both levelly. "I don't deny being a farmer's son. As I get older I see more and more that my father, for all his simple birth, was a nobler man than many at this court. Particularly the two examples I see before me."

Edred, his face flushed, leaned towards the bars. "Watch your tongue, Belasko, or someone will have it out."

Belasko's hand flashed out quicker than thought and caught the front of Edred's shirt through the cell bars. He pulled, slamming the adviser into the bars with enough force to blow the breath out of his lungs.

"Careful there," Belasko said, voice dangerously quiet. "You wouldn't want to go making threats you can't back up, would you?" Edred struggled against Belasko's grip, but Belasko's hold was firm as steel. "Don't you worry. I know what I am." He let go just as Edred pushed against the bars, sending him stumbling back. "I know what I am, and I know what you are. Now begone. I think I've had quite enough of you visitors today."

Edred edged away, back to the wall, before turning and stumbling back down the corridor. Viktor eyed Belasko with an angry, disgusted look on his face. "Oh, we know what you are," hissed the steward. "We know just what you are. We came by to tell you, make sure you understood, whatever rank you held, whatever privileges, all that is done. You came from nothing, to nothing will you return." He grimaced, spat on the floor in front of Belasko, then turned and stalked after his colleague.

Belasko leaned against the bars, calling out, "Oh, and gentlemen? If you find more stimulating company out there, could you please send them in? It's quite boring here with only rats for visitors."

He slumped down onto his pallet, head in his hands. *Oh God, it just gets worse.*

His thoughts turned once again to the past.

Shortly after dawn on that long ago day, the enemy showed signs of breaking camp. Belasko edged backwards into the pass, keeping behind rocks and shrubs in an attempt to make sure he wasn't observed, before he turned and made his way back to the narrowest point, the switchback. He positioned himself just the other side of it. He was close enough to the corner that anyone who turned it would be within reach of his blade, and he of theirs, but would not have time to draw a bow, or bring a longer weapon like a spear or halberd to bear. He was going to have to rely on speed. He tried to relax the tension in his muscles, breathing deeply to calm his racing heart.

He could hear them long before they reached the switchback. The trudge of many feet echoed from the cliff walls, the laughter and chatter of soldiers that are sure they are safe in their numbers and conventional wisdom. Who would send scouts into the Dellan pass? Surely no one would attempt to move troops through it.

It's a good thing our generals are paranoid.

The sound of feet on the rocky ground drew closer, then slowed as the enemy soldiers went single file. The first of them rounded the corner, stopping when he saw Belasko.

"Wha—" he said, surprise flashing across his face, but Belasko's blade flashed faster. He took out the man's throat before he could finish the word. He fell to his knees, blood running between the fingers that clutched at his ruined neck, then tumbling forwards. Dead.

All this had taken fractions of a second, and the next of the Baskan soldiers rounded the corner. Belasko's blade flashed again in the morning sun, his bloody work begun in earnest.

It was some time later. Belasko wasn't sure how much later, as he had lost all sense of time, his world shrinking to the few feet of rocky ground in front of him. A pile of dead opponents lay before him. The enemy soldiers had stopped coming. He was glad of the rest, stretching his muscles and taking a sip of water from his canteen.

"Hello there!" a voice called from around the corner. "May we have permission to retrieve our dead?"

"I'm of a mind to say no, as having to climb over them will hamper the rest of your men, but I'm not one to disrespect the dead," Belasko replied. "But no tricks. Anyone that comes around that corner will join them."

"Fair enough," said the voice. "We'll just pull them back from here, alright?"

A few moments later, the corpses started to disappear backwards, pulled around the corner of the pass by their ankles. This went on for some while before the pass was a little clearer. The bodies that had fallen fully on Belasko's side of the switchback remained untouched.

"Listen," came the voice again, "I would see the man I speak with, who has killed so many of my soldiers today. Do I have your permission to approach?"

Belasko thought on this before he replied. "Okay. But you

come alone, and no tricks. I meant what I said before. Try anything and you'll be dead before you know it."

"That sounds fair to me. I'm coming now."

A few moments later a man rounded the corner, blinking in surprise at how quickly Belasko's blade appeared at his throat. He met Belasko's gaze calmly and raised an eyebrow. "No tricks. I just want to talk."

Belasko nodded. "That's fair enough, but the blade stays where it is."

They looked at each other, each taking in the other's appearance. *This one's got rank,* Belasko thought to himself. *Look at that fancy uniform. Lots of shiny buttons.* The other man was older, salt and pepper hair to go with the wrinkles around his eyes, and the typical olive skin of a Baskan. He had an air of authority about him, as if he was used to command, to men and women following his orders without question. He regarded Belasko quizzically. "What sort of a man are you, to stand alone against so many?"

Belasko shrugged, aware that his opponent would feel the movement through the blade held to his throat. "What sort of man am I? I'm a Villanese soldier. A farmer's son. As for standing alone, my compatriots are behind me. I just asked if I could have first crack at you."

The Baskan officer chuckled. "Well, if you're a typical Villanese soldier then I should take my soldiers home because the war is already lost." He squinted at Belasko. "No, I think you're a rarer sort. But no matter how quick your sword arm is, you will eventually tire. When you do, my men will overwhelm you. Why don't you just let us pass."

"You know the answer to that. I'm a soldier, sworn to protect my country. This side of the pass is sovereign Villanese territory. I cannot let enemy soldiers through it. I won't stand down, just as you won't retreat. So you're just going to have to keep sending your troops to die, one by one. If I grow tired, if I fall, one of my comrades-in-arms will come forward to take my place."

The Baskan officer smiled. "This may be true, what you say, but I think you are here alone, whether or not there are others on their way. Listen, you seem an honourable sort, and you are just defending your country, as you say. There is perhaps another way to solve our dilemma. You Villanese keep to the ways of the duelling circle, do you not? To settle disagreements?"

What is he up to? "That we do. I believe that Baskan law is similar."

"That it is. What I suggest is this: a duel. A duel to settle our impasse. You against a champion of my choosing. If you defeat them, my forces will leave and find another way through the mountains. If they defeat you... Well, our way will be clear, won't it?"

Belasko eyed the officer warily. The other man smiled. "No tricks, I promise."

"Can I think about it?"

"You can, but not for too long or the offer will be withdrawn."

"I tell you what, if I can hold this pass until the hour before nightfall, then I'll face your champion. How does that sound?"

"It sounds like madness. Do you really feel like you can hold until then?"

"I can and I will. If I hold the pass until the hour before nightfall then I will face your champion. I'll probably need a rest by then, so I'll face them at sundown. What do you say?"

The officer shrugged. "On your own head be it. Literally, most likely. I'll return to my lines now and send my men forward once more. If you survive until the hour before nightfall I will grant you an hour's rest, and then you will face my champion. It seems foolish to me."

"Oh, I agree. Foolish to send so many Baskans to die."

The officer walked backwards around the corner, eyes on Belasko all the while. Soon the sound of horns could be heard and the Baskans started their advance once more. The Baskans tried all manner of strategies in an attempt to surprise him, to catch him out. Attacking with two blades at once, coming around the corner with blades held at odd heights and angles. Nothing they tried worked, and Belasko fought on.

To Belasko in those next few hours it seemed as if time had stopped; that he had always been in this narrow rocky space, killing and killing and killing again. Although he had been practicing for this moment, drilling with his comrades, nothing could really have prepared him for the shock of taking another's life. Of ending all that they were. He felt numb, as if part of himself was closing off to the world. The world that faded away until all that was left was that which fell within the reach of his sword.

He was weary, his limbs heavy and burning with fatigue, but he could not stop, could not slow down, or he would die. The Baskan soldiers slowed though, increasingly reluctant to come forward and face this demon that had taken so many of their fellows. He could sense it. He could feel their trepidation.

Eventually he became aware that it was getting darker. Then the horns blew once more and the advance stopped. A familiar voice called around the corner.

"You've done it, Lords of the Deep know how. May I approach?"

Belasko cleared his throat. "Is it that time already? My, how time flies. Of course, approach."

The Baskan officer appeared around the corner, stepping over his dead soldiers. He shook his head, stopping as Belasko's blade once more flashed to rest at his throat. He arched an eyebrow. "You really don't give up, do you? You have an hour to rest and prepare yourself, then you will face my champion — if you wish to carry on with our agreement?"

Belasko nodded.

"Good. If you don't mind, we'll collect our dead. You can come around to our side of the pass. My soldiers are under orders to leave you unharmed. They are also ordered not to advance, so you can rest knowing you have done your duty."

"Thank you, but I'll stay here. Blow one of your horns when it's time, and I'll come face your champion."

The officer nodded, and withdrew. Belasko relaxed a little, wincing at the fiery ache in muscles that had been worked hard and weren't happy about it. He couldn't think of anything in his training that had prepared him for the endurance he had needed today. He felt exhausted, worn thin, his whole body tight and twitchy, muscles fluttering on the edge of cramp. Belasko grimaced as he began to stretch, attempting to ease the discomfort as best he could.

The next visitor to his cell a few hours later was the same sandy-haired inquisitor he had seen the previous night. The inquisitor walked up to his cell as Belasko completed a round of exercises. He ignored him, concentrating on his movements, feeling the pull and push of his muscles at work as he ran through the set of moves designed to practice and ready the body for unarmed combat. When he reached the end of the set he slowed, turning his focus towards the inquisitor and bowing, as if towards an opponent.

The inquisitor laughed, clapping in mock appreciation. "Oh very good, Belasko. I see you remember old Markus's teachings well enough. You've added some additions of your own, I see. It's to be expected after all this time."

The mention of his old fencing master's name, the previous king's champion, surprised Belasko. He peered again at the inquisitor, who was retrieving a small three-legged stool from an alcove in the wall behind him. A shock of recognition passed through him.

"Ervan?"

The inquisitor held up the stool before sitting on it. "You know, I'm amazed that these seem to be standard issue outside every cell. Every cell in the dungeons. I suspect someone in the palace has a relative with a surprisingly profitable business making stools." He settled on the stool, turning his attention back to Belasko. "Yes, it's me. Ervan. Been a while, hasn't it?"

Belasko nodded. "I'll say. It's been years. Not since..."

Ervan gave him a cold smile. "That's right, not since... Well." He gestured to his eye patch. "You know, it's bad enough to lose an eye in a fencing match, but when one's fellow students don't even pay you a visit when you're recuperating... that hurt. That truly hurt."

"We tried to visit you, Ervan, we really did. Your family wouldn't let us in. They didn't want common soldiers in their house. Then afterwards, we thought you didn't want to see us, to be reminded..." Belasko sighed. "I'm sorry. We were younger then, and thoughtless. We should have made more of an effort."

Ervan stared at him, single eye gleaming. "Yes, you should." He leaned forward on his stool. "You know, before you came along I was Markus's favourite. I was the one who should have been his successor. Instead you took my eye *and* my future."

Belasko's mind flashed back to that day, years ago. The ring of practice blades, a lunge, the shock of brittle metal breaking, blood flowing. He shook his head. "I'm sorry, more than you can know. But the blade broke. It was an accident. If I hadn't reacted quickly, pulled my blow, you'd have died. I know your mother blamed Markus's school, blamed me."

Ervan continued, ignoring him. "I've followed your career closely, Belasko. Watched the humble farmer's son, hero of the Last War, become the king's champion. Raised up above so many others. I've seen what you've done with your Academy. So much more ambitious than Markus's old fencing studio, eh? I've seen you building a force of fighters, training them, sending them out into royal service — but all still loyal to you. And I've seen you. Arrogant, looking down your nose at your betters. Time for you to fall a peg or two, Belasko. Time for you to fall."

A long silence stretched out between them.

Eventually Belasko broke it. "I don't recognise myself in what you say. My Academy was built out of loyalty to my king, to better train his officers and soldiers, for any that sought it and showed aptitude, be they farmers' sons or the children of noble houses. Like yourself. How is it you came to work in the Inquisition? You surely don't need the money."

"I too serve out of loyalty, Belasko, loyalty to my king and country. And I will see you hang."

Belasko laughed. "How good of the Inquisition to provide an investigator that assigns blame before their investigation is complete. I am innocent, Ervan, as I'm sure you know."

"I know no such thing. You profess innocence now, but we have found a letter in the king's apartments. It was unopened, delivered the night of the prince's death. A letter in which you profess guilt for your actions, begging for forgiveness that you know will never come."

"That's... that's impossible. I wrote no such letter, it has to be a forgery." Belasko paled. "It has to be. Let me see it. Let me see it and I will prove it to you."

Ervan snorted. "Let you lay hands on a critical piece of evidence? I think not. Besides the letter, we know that you visited the cook you had placed in the kitchens while she worked on the dish that was poisoned. Enough people in the palace can attest to your reflexes. It would have been easy work for you to slip something into the food without anyone noticing. No, I rather think we have things sewn up. The only question is, why?"

"That's not the only question, you bloody idiot, but if you

ask it you'll realise it can't be answered. Because I didn't do it. I'm loyal to the king, to the royal family, and I loved Kellan like a brother. Like. A. Brother. I would never have done anything to harm him. Even if all that wasn't true, I would never stoop to using poison. That's the work of a coward, and for all my faults I have never been accused of cowardice."

Ervan smiled, a cold, hungry smile. "You can rant and rave all you like, but we will find you guilty. You will hang. And you will confess first."

"Good luck with that."

Ervan stood, putting his stool back in its alcove.

Belasko tried another tack. "Look, you don't like me, that much is clear. But you know that I am an honourable man. You are an officer of his majesty's Inquisition, pledged to uphold the law and root out truth. I have been framed. I don't know why, but I will help you get to the truth. Let me talk to the king, he'll see the sense in my words, and we can catch the prince's killer together. Just let me talk to the king."

Ervan laughed. "Catch the killer together? You'd like that, wouldn't you? Why do you always have to be the hero, Belasko? Not this time. Not this time. There's more chance of me seeing out of my missing eye than of you seeing the king, let alone pleading your case. No, your time is over. You should have stayed on your father's farm. Or died at Dellan Pass."

Belasko had passed the granted hour gently stretching out the muscles he had put to such hard use that day. Then he rested, trying to martial what energy he had left. The hour passed, the horn blew, and he walked through the switchback to face his destiny.

As he emerged into the widening valley that held the Baskan forces, he stopped, taking in the sight before him. An army was arrayed further back in the valley than he had previously observed, granting space for the duel to occur. Every Baskan soldier's eye was on him as he emerged. The sun was low on the horizon behind them, the enemy troops silhouetted against it as it cast a golden glow over their numbers, shadows stretching long across the rocky terrain. Some way in front of the army stood the officer, talking with some of his men. A lone figure was off to one side, stripped to the waist, stretching and warming up. A duelling circle had been marked on the floor of the valley by the simple expedient of arranging some of the rocks with which the area was so abundantly blessed.

The soldiers stopped and waited in silence as he approached, their stony faces at first implacable. Belasko became aware of muttering among the Baskan forces, as those at the front relayed a description of him to those behind. He could hear sounds of disbelief, one cry of "he ain't that big!" which was quickly hushed. He met the gaze of the front rank head on and while he saw open dislike in their eyes there was also grudging respect. Belasko paused, standing to attention and offering his opponents a salute. A murmur passed through the crowd before the gesture was returned by the entire Baskan force.

The officer came forward to greet him, despite the disapproval his fellows showed as a low rumble of dissent spread through their ranks.

"General," one of them said, "be careful. I wouldn't—"

The officer snorted. "What? Risk yourself? No, I'm sure you wouldn't. This man could have killed me twice today and didn't, so I think I can trust him. There is something of honour between combatants." He smiled as Belasko drew near.

"General? I supposed I should have guessed, what with all the shiny buttons on your uniform."

The general chuckled. "Oh yes, we do like to make ourselves stand out. What is your name? I would know the name of the man who has frustrated my plans." He held out a hand.

Belasko clasped his hand and shook it. "Belasko. My name is Belasko."

"Belasko. I am General Edyard." Belasko's eyes widened. The general laughed again. "Oh, you've heard of me."

"Yes sir, you're the commander of the Baskan army."

"I am, I am. Although maybe not for much longer, after today. You've quite ruined what was supposed to be my boldest plan yet."

"I wish I could say that I'm sorry."

"I know. You're doing your duty — as were my soldiers that died today. For better or ill, I am a man of my word, and this matter will be decided now. Are you ready?"

Belasko nodded. "I am. Is that your champion?" He indicated the man who had been stretching and now made his way to the duelling circle.

"It is. I warn you, he's never been defeated."

Belasko smiled. "Neither have I."

General Edyard nodded. "Have you fought many duels?"

Belasko started to walk towards the duelling circle. "None," he called back over his shoulder, "but now seems as good a time as any to start."

Belasko followed his opponent's example by stripping to the waist, then both combatants took their places across from each other, although neither yet entered the circle. Once they crossed the line there would be no going back; they would fight to the death.

Belasko's opponent was tall and heavily muscled, wielding a large broadsword which he swung from side to side in a sweeping motion. His head was shaved and his torso boasted many scars. He frowned at Belasko. "Don't you need to warm up?" he asked.

Belasko shrugged. "I've been practicing all day." He drew his sword, nodding to the Baskan. "Ready?"

"Ready," the other man said. They bowed to each other and entered the circle.

It's fair to say that Belasko was not at his best. He had been fighting all day, on top of a sleepless night, and he was exhausted. His opponent, on the other hand, was fresh. Rested. He lashed out with an overhand sweep, which Belasko avoided by diving clumsily out of the way. In fact whatever his opponent tried, Belasko just got out of the way, until it seemed like the Baskan champion was chasing him around the circle, much to the amusement of the troops.

He stopped, growling at Belasko. "Why don't you fight? Try your sword against mine!"

Belasko only smiled. "I'll raise my sword when I need to, not before."

The Baskan, frustrated, swung for Belasko once more. Belasko twisted out of his way and the champion turned to follow. As he did so he turned right into the light of the setting sun. The Baskan blinked, momentarily blinded, and that's when Belasko struck. His sword flickered out and the real fight began.

His opponent almost didn't see the blow coming and reacted slowly, only just managing to get his blade up to block Belasko's. The Baskan tried to step to the side, turn Belasko around, so that he wasn't squinting into the sun, but the Villanese farmer's son was relentless. Striking first at one side and then another, keeping his big Baskan opponent right where he wanted him. Belasko knew that what strength remained to him wouldn't last long. He launched a furious attack, reeling off blow after blow, thrusts and strikes from all angles and heights. His opponent stumbled backwards against the onslaught but still managed to block whatever Belasko tried. Then, as he retreated, the Baskan champion's heel caught on a rock protruding from the valley floor and he fell backwards, arms spreading wide. Defences open.

Belasko made a desperate lunge inside his opponent's reach and the tip of his blade took another Baskan throat. Overbalanced, Belasko fell with his opponent who, in his dying moments, tried to bring his own blade back to bear. Now, robbed of strength, his blow scored Belasko's side as they both hit the ground hard.

The Baskan emitted a gurgling noise, twitching slightly as his blood pumped out onto both the valley floor and Belasko. He rolled off his opponent, staggering to his feet, something he achieved on the second attempt and only by leaning on his sword. He saluted his dying opponent and, clutching his bleeding side, turned to face General Edyard and his troops.

The Baskan forces had fallen silent, looking on at the gore-covered Belasko in dismay, and as he turned to face them, horns could be heard in the distance — from the other side of the pass.

"See? I told you," Belasko called out. "My brothers and sisters in arms were right behind me."

"A penny for your thoughts?"

He opened his eyes and scrabbled to his feet, heart racing. *Someone approaching should have woken me*. Belasko wiped his hands across his eyes, then bowed when he saw the slight figure that stood in front of his cell, long blonde hair almost glowing in the dim torchlight.

"Princess, my apologies. I was daydreaming. Somewhere along the way I appear to have dozed off."

She smiled, though she looked at him with sad eyes. "What were you dreaming of? My offer still holds: a penny for your thoughts."

"I'm not sure they're worth a penny. Some visitors earlier, they made me think... of events long ago. Of Dellan Pass."

She tilted her head to one side. "Ah. The day that made you a legend."

"Ha. Legend? Hardly. I was lucky that day, and have been lucky since. Until now."

"Yes. We are all of us unlucky now." She looked away.

Damn me, how could I be so insensitive?

"Princess Lilliana, I'm so sorry. More than I can say. But you have to believe me, I had nothing to do with..." Belasko trailed off, finding it difficult to say the words, as if voicing his implication in the prince's death would make it true. "I loved Kellan. We were close. I could never do anything to hurt him, any more than I could hurt you or your father. I am sworn to protect your house. You know this."

She turned back to him, eyes wet, her fresh grief running off her cold as a mountain stream. Still, she stood straight. *We forget sometimes, with her quiet nature and bookish ways, but this one has a core of iron.*

A memory came to him then, from years before. The day he had been raised to the position of king's champion. A celebration had been made in his honour. A feast, with dancing to follow. It should have been a moment of triumph, but at the dance, which as the guest of honour he was supposed to lead, none of the ladies of the court would deign to dance with him — a commoner. Shamed in front of everyone, the evening turning into a disaster, a small hand alighted on his arm. The princess. Only a child. "Would you dance with me, Belasko? Everyone else is dreadfully dull." She had pulled him onto the dance floor and they had whirled, careless of the form of the dance, whooping with laughter. It broke the tension and saved the evening.

Lilliana spoke, bringing him back to the present. "I know this. I know all of this. Just as I know that if you wanted someone dead it would be with blades drawn, not poison. Whatever evidence the Inquisition has found, I'm sure it can be explained, if one was to dig a little deeper." She paused. "Which makes me wonder why the Inquisition are not digging any deeper. Why they are accepting what little evidence they have."

Belasko sighed. "Ervan, the inquisitor leading the investigation. He... let's say he has little love for me. Thinks I have risen too high, wants to bring me down a peg or three."

Lilliana frowned, nose wrinkling in thought. "No, it's not that. Or at least, not only that. I think there's something deeper going on and it frightens me." She shook her head, as if chasing her thoughts away. "Enough of that for now. How are you? Your foot, the ache in your joints?" She smiled as he gawped at her. "What, you thought I didn't know? Father tells me much. I thought he would tell me more now that I am heir..." Her voice trailed off before returning with strength. "He has told me what you have told him, of your fears that your body is failing you. Of your desire to find your replacement and retire. I must say that you appear undiminished to outside eyes."

Belasko regarded her for a moment. When he spoke again it was with a quiet voice. "Thank you for your concern, your highness. Outside eyes cannot see what I feel. I won't lie, the damp conditions, the cold, neither are good for what ails me. The pain in my foot troubles me almost constantly, the ache in my joints flaring up to join it on occasion. I fear — have feared for a while — that I will fail your father, as my body begins to fail me. I have been searching for a protégé, someone who could eventually replace me, but so far I have yet to find one I would trust with your lives. Not when it counted. But now," Belasko gestured around him, "someone would see my life's work undone, and my life with it." He moved to the bars, clutching them fiercely and pressing his forehead to the cold steel "I did not harm your brother, your highness, and I would not die for whoever did so. Please, take word to your father the king. I must speak to him. Surely he can see that none of this makes sense?"

Lilliana reached through the bars to touch the side of his face with a gentle hand, and as she did so that shock of memory returned and ran through him. The princess as a young girl, dancing with him at the ball, laughing as he whirled her around and around. The memory left him as she began to speak.

"Dear Belasko, I will do what I can. Father is almost mad with grief and rage. He sees almost no one. When I have seen him these last days it is almost always in the presence of others. I will try to see him alone and plead your case. If it is within my power, I will bring him to see you. Whatever happens, I will intercede on your behalf. Know that to be true." She looked back down the corridor before turning to him once more. "For now, I must go. The guard will only look the other way for a few moments. My father would be unhappy if he knew that I had come to see you. Peace Belasko, know that there is at least one person in the palace that believes in you. I will try to visit you again, when I can." She leant forward, placed a delicate kiss on his brow between the bars, and went to leave. She hesitated, turning back. "You know, it isn't just for your skill with a blade that my father has kept you close, raised you up? It is your heart as well. Your character." With that, she was gone.

Belasko stood for a long time with his head against the bars, taking deep shuddering breaths.

4

A fist crashed into Belasko's cheekbone, snapping his head to one side and rocking him against the restraints tied at elbow, wrist, knee and ankle. They held him in the chair that had been brought into his cell that morning, bolted into previously unseen notches in the floor.

"Think you can kill Prince Kellan and get away with it? Think anyone will believe you if you cry innocence?"

Another blow, this time to his stomach. Air blew out of his lungs and he hunched forwards, spittle and bile coughed up from his split and bleeding lips.

"Think anyone cares about you?"

Another blow to his ribs. Belasko thought he felt one snap, sharp pain spreading through the dull ache that his side had become. One of his two visitors leaned down, cupping his chin in one big hand and tilting his eyes up to meet theirs. The two men that had brought the chair were big bruisers, used to dealing out pain to those that couldn't fight back. They both wore the black of the Inquisition, but in cheap cloth and without Ervan's symbols of rank.

The man that had been working him over sighed, dropping

Belasko's chin as he turned to his colleague. "Still no give. Fancy a go? I'll give my knuckles a rest." As he said this he plunged his hands into a bucket of ice-filled water. He was the taller of the two, dark-haired, with a nose that had clearly been broken more than once.

They had been at it for most of the morning, taking it in turns, trying to get him to admit to some part in the murder of Prince Kellan. So far their work had been fruitless.

"Innocent," whispered Belasko.

The second man paused in the process of binding his knuckles. "What was that?" he asked. This one was shorter than his fellow, but no less powerfully built. Squat, with flame-coloured hair and a squint.

Belasko looked up at him. "I'm innocent." His voice was hoarse from yelling the same thing for most of that morning. "I did not kill the prince."

The shorter man snorted, and resumed preparing himself for Belasko's continued beating. "That's the sort of thing a guilty man would say."

"Or an innocent one." Belasko tried to smile through his bruises, but his face was too swollen. He turned his head and spat some of the blood that was filling his mouth. He heard a rattling sound when it hit the floor of his cell. *Damn, I think that was a tooth.*

"No, no, no," the taller man was saying, probing his misshapen nose with a crooked forefinger. "That's not how it works. You're guilty. We keep hitting you until you admit it. *That's* how this works."

"Bring the king. I must see the king. I'm innocent."

The second man bent down to him. "Oh yeah, we'll just fetch the king. He loves popping down to the cells for a chat with murdering scum." He snorted with laughter. "He's always coming down here, is his majesty. Now, the sooner you admit your guilt, the sooner this'll all be over.

There'll be no need to move on to your friends and family."

Belasko looked up as sharply as his injuries would allow. The man grinned down at him. "That's right. If you don't see sense and admit your guilt, we'll have to start hurting people who're close to you. See if that doesn't jog your memory. What's his name, that guy that works for you? Lawrence, something like that? Your students too, from that fancy Academy. Men, women, we're not fussy. They might be good with a blade but they'll not be cut out for this. I reckon they'll squeal good. In the end ..."

"Don't you touch them, you animals! Don't you bloody touch them!" Belasko's voice tore, ragged in his throat.

The red-haired man turned to his taller colleague. "Hear that? How many men do you think he's killed in his life, the great Belasko? And he calls us animals."

"I've never tied someone down and beaten them. I've always faced my enemies like a man."

"Oh ho, he's a defiant one, isn't he? We'll see how long that lasts." The shorter man looked him over for a moment. Then he raised one of his big hobnailed boots and brought it crashing down on Belasko's bad foot. The duellist grunted, biting his lip hard to stop from screaming. "Oh yes. We'll see how long that lasts."

The bucket of water was thrown over him, waking him in the process. Belasko blinked through swollen eyelids as the men undid his bindings and tumbled him onto his pallet. He could dimly make them out as they unbolted the chair from the floor and left, locking the cell door behind them. He could hear their conversation as it faded down the tunnel.

"Tough man, that one. Was still mumbling about being innocent right up until he passed out."

"Reckon he is?"

Laughter. "Yeah, right. Don't care much either way – not what we're paid for."

"I know, I know. Reckon the king'll come to see him?"

"Yeah, the king'll come. Just as soon as I start shitting gold."

Then the creak and slam of the outer door, the clank of bolts shooting home as it was locked.

The king will come. He has to. The king will come.

Belasko passed in and out of consciousness as he waited through the night for King Mallor to come. His dreams were fitful, disturbed things, full of faces from long ago mixed up with current friends, all staring at him accusingly. Fingers pointed, blame bestowed. Prince Kellan, face purple and swollen, mumbling around a tongue that lolled out of his mouth. "Why'd you do it, Belasko? Why'd you kill me?" In Belasko's dream the prince regarded him with sad eyes as carrion creatures tore at his flesh.

"I didn't kill you!" Belasko screamed. 'I didn't!"

The prince shook his head. "Well someone did, and everyone's saying it was you. They can't all be wrong."

"I didn't do it! I didn't!"

Then he dreamed of his childhood on the farm. His mother and father, quiet, gentle people, who uncomplaining got on with the never-ending toil of running a mountain smallholding. He was helping his father dig a hole for a fencepost. Hard, dirty work. His father smiled at him, wiping the sweat from his brow and smearing it with dirt in the process. "It's hard work son, but honest. There're worse things a man can do. Much worse."

His father went to wipe his brow again, but in an instant was gone, replaced by the recruiting sergeant that had visited their family farm when he was fifteen. He rattled off a perfect salute to the young Belasko. The recruiter, splendid in his uniform, buttons gleaming, smiled at Belasko. "Looks like hard work, that. Surely a likely lad such as yourself can do something better? Why not serve your king, your country? The army needs promising young men like you."

Then the recruiter was gone, replaced by other dreams in which he saw everything he had built come crashing down. His Academy burned to ashes, his friends' lives ruined as they were marched through the streets in chains. All turned to him with accusing eyes. "Why, Belasko? Why have you abandoned us?" they asked.

Belasko woke, coughing. He looked about him wildly. A dim light came through the grate near the ceiling of his cell. Dawn. Another day. The king still hadn't come.

5

It was then that Belasko's thoughts turned to escape. He had been holding on to the hope that his innocence alone would be enough, that those who suspected him would see the error of their ways. That the king — in recognition of Belasko's service, if not out of a belief in his innocence — would come and see him. That the king seemingly believed him guilty hurt as much as any physical injury he now carried. His grief at the loss of Prince Kellan, was doubled by the loss of King Mallor's regard.

He looked around, wincing at the pain that lanced through him at even this simple movement, taking in once again the space of his confinement, looking for anything he could use to make good an escape. *Nothing.* He shook his head, disgusted. He knew from previous examination that the grill was far too small for him to get through, even if he were somehow able to remove the grill itself. Likewise the bars were set too solidly in the floor and ceiling. They could not be budged. Not without many hours of work with tools and time he didn't have. *There has to be a way.*

When it arrived, help came from an unlikely source.

Belasko had been dozing fitfully, waking occasionally to stretch and try to sooth his injuries as best he could. A voice startled him out of his rest.

"Oh Belasko, what have they done to you?" It was Princess Lilliana.

Belasko swung his feet off his pallet and struggled to rise. "More importantly, what haven't they done to me? Two of Ervan's men paid me a visit, beat me, tried force a confession out of me. They haven't done any permanent damage. Everything you see will heal, in time."

"So either they don't have permission to hurt you further, or are holding back."

He nodded, wincing at the sequence of pains that set off. "Holding worse punishments in reserve. That's a pleasant thought."

"Then it's a good thing I paid you a visit. Here." Lilliana moved up to the bars of his cell, removing something from under her cloak and passing it through to him. A plain leather satchel, the sort that priests or scribes might carry. Belasko opened it, peering inside at its contents. It held cloth, and something shiny on top.

"What is this?" he asked, squinting as he retrieved the shining object. "And how did you smuggle it in?"

Lilliana laughed, raising an eyebrow. "You think the guards would dare to search me?"

"Fair point," he grunted. "Still, you took a risk even in coming back." His fumbling hands closed on the metal and withdrew a key. He looked down at it for a moment and then sharply up at the princess. "What is this?"

She smiled. "A key, idiot — what does it look like? More specifically, a skeleton key that will open many of the doors in the palace, including your cell door and the door into the guardroom at the end of the corridor."

"How did you get this?"

"It is part of a set that my father's steward keeps in his office. I overheard he and my father talking about them one day, when they thought I had my head in a book. I managed to talk my way into his office and lay my hands on it while pretending to look something up in the previous stewards' records. A discrepancy in the palace archives caught my attention that I desperately needed to clarify, or so I told them. There is also a hooded robe, one that should make you into a passable priest. I use it when I want to travel through the city unrecognised. Only a few members of my personal guard know about it, so you shouldn't be spotted."

"This is... unexpected, your highness. I will admit I'm surprised at how accustomed you seem to be to this sort of intrigue. I take it you are helping me escape, not asking me to take part in some mummer's play?"

"Intrigue? When you grow up a princess, always watched, you soon discover ways to find yourself a little freedom." Lilliana shook her head. "I want to help you get out of here. I believe in your innocence, even if everyone else seems willing to accept the idea that you're guilty." Her face hardened. "Every moment you spend in here is a moment my brother's killer is enjoying their freedom. I don't much like that idea. So get out of here and prove your innocence. Find the real killer. Can you do that?"

Belasko dropped to one knee, bowing his head. "I swear on my life and honour, I will find your brother's killer and bring them to justice."

She nodded, satisfied but still grim. "Good. I wouldn't expect anything less. Now get up, you're in a bad enough way without adding to your bruises on that stone floor. The disguise and key will do you no good without a plan. Here is what I have worked out. Tell me what you think."

~

A few hours later, having waited for the noon bell, Belasko found himself waiting outside the door to the guard room, hand resting on the door handle. The cells were in the basement of a large, round tower. The guard's room beyond was the hub at the centre of the basements, the corridors of cells leading off from it like the spokes of a wheel. This design, along with a sliding viewing panel in the door to each corridor, meant that few guards were needed to keep watch over all the prisoners. Two guards were regularly stationed there at any one time and, fortunately for Belasko, the viewing panel for his corridor remained closed.

The princess had found out from one of her own guards, who complained of having the same duty in years past, that the cell guards took it in turns to fetch their midday meal. The first guard — the one loyal to the princess, who had turned a blind eye to her visit — had left to collect her food after the various palace bells had finished tolling the midday chimes.

Belasko had, as swiftly and quietly as possible, used the key the princess had given him to open his cell, not yet locking it behind him. By Belasko's estimation, he had around ten minutes before the other guard returned, so had to work quickly. He had padded up to the guard room door and placed the key gently in the lock.

Belasko exploded into motion, turning the key and slamming the door open in one quick movement. As he burst into the room, he flung the satchel the princess had given him at the surprised guard at the centre of the room, who did not even have time to get out of his chair. The guard lifted an arm to bat aside the satchel, and Belasko followed, stepping up to him and slamming his hands closed in a tight grip around the man's throat. Belasko began to squeeze.

Panic shot through the guard's eyes and he thrashed around, trying to escape Belasko's steel grip. He scrabbled at his hands, but the duellist would not be deterred.

"Hush," Belasko said, "I'm not going to kill you, just send you to sleep for a bit." His hands felt out the arteries at either side of the guard's neck and applied pressure. The guard continued to struggle for a few moments, until his eyes rolled up and his head started to loll. Belasko bundled the guard into the corridor to his cell. He hissed at the pain from his broken rib as he moved the guard, gasping and trying to avoid breathing too deeply.

"Sorry about that," he said to the unconscious guard, as he used some cord Lilliana had supplied to bind him. "Nothing personal."

"God's blood!" Belasko swore as he lifted him onto the pallet, pain flaring through his chest, before throwing the tatty blanket that had kept him warm at night over the guard. Belasko went out, locking the cell behind him, and headed back into the guardroom, also locking the door to the corridor. He retrieved the satchel, withdrew the robe from it and pulled it on over his clothes. He raised the hood and made his way up the stairs that ran up the wall of the guardroom. Opening the door at the top, he carefully checked to make sure that the coast was clear, then snuck out of the guardroom and into the palace beyond.

He had a few minutes yet before the other guard returned and raised the alarm. Hopefully she would wonder where her fellow guard was for a while before thinking to check Belasko's cell. If she didn't inspect the apparently slumbering form on the pallet, Belasko might have more precious minutes to make good his escape.

Fortunately for him, the tower that contained the dungeons was close to the curtain wall of the palace grounds, and a number of the lesser gates to bridges that led out into the city proper. Belasko breathed a sigh of relief when he realised that it was a petition day, when the palace was open to the public to petition the king or his functionaries about the issues that mattered to them, no matter how petty. Those who had been seen or failed to gain an audience were leaving the palace with minimal checks.

He went to join their number, hoping to take a place in the middle of the crowd as they made their way to the nearest gate. But as he took a step out of the shadow, a heavy hand fell on his shoulder.

"Now what business does a priest have down in the cells?" a female voice asked. The hand on his shoulder turned him around to face a young, stocky woman in a spotless guard's uniform. "Though I dare say there's a few sinners down there that could do with a bit of salvation."

Belasko kept his head down, hood pulled low. His heart sank as he realised that this was the second cell guard returning with the midday meal.

"Not in the cells, ma'am," Belasko said, affecting the voice of much older man. "I'm looking for the chapel in St Ketura's tower. I seem to have got turned around. Forgive me, I've not visited the palace before."

The guard smiled. "It is quite a maze, isn't it?" She released Belasko's shoulder and stepped out of the lee of the tower. "You're not too far off track." The guard pointed to a tower a little further along the broad way that ran inside the curtain wall. "That's the one you're looking for. Good day to you, Father."

"And you ma'am, thank you for your help." Belasko raised his hand in benediction. "May the saints and Aronos himself bless you for this kindness."

The guard laughed and waved him away, turning to go back into the tower. After the door closed behind her Belasko moved swiftly. Ignoring the guard's directions, head down, he set off in the direction of the nearest gate and bridge as fast as he could without arousing suspicion. Heart pounding, he knew he had minutes at best. His escape attempt could be over before it began.

Belasko joined the flow of people leaving the palace, working his way into the middle of the crowd, as far from the guards stationed at either side of the gate as he could.

Come on, nearly there.

He was in the centre of the crowd now, the press of people carrying him forward. Drawing level with the gates, the guards to either side looked bored, waving people through with barely a second glance. Then, from behind him he heard shouting.

"...the alarm, raise the alarm! Someone's escaped from the cells. Close the gates! Raise the alarm!" It was the voice of the guard he had just bumped into. Belasko resisted the temptation to turn around, although several in the crowd were attempting to stop and do just that. However, the mass of the crowd pushed them forward, as people started to rush for the gates. No one wanted to get caught up in whatever was happening.

Belasko heard other guards taking up the cry along the palace walls. The two on his gate looked at each other, yelling, trying to be heard above the crowd. They both stepped forward, trying to stop the flow of traffic. They might as well have tried to stop the sea. There was nothing they could do against that weight of people, and both were pushed back.

The gates behind them started to swing closed, struggling against the tide of bodies, but the heavy mechanisms in the gatehouse kept turning, and people were pushing and shoving now, desperate to get through the narrowing gap.

Belasko was helped by his position. The guards that had been trying to keep them all back were gone now, overrun and trampled, and he was pushed towards the closing gates by the throng. He got to them just as they were closing, squeezing through the narrow gap as he felt the rough wood tear and clutch at him. He pushed himself forward, launching off some unfortunate soul who fell back through the gates, and he stumbled through just as they slammed shut behind him, one of the last to make it through.

There were guards shouting down from the walls at him and the rest of the crowd to stop, to wait, but they were ignored as those that escaped passed over the bridge and dissipated into the city beyond. While Belasko had his own reasons, it seemed no one wanted to be caught up in whatever madness had infected the palace.

Belasko made his way away from the palace as quickly as he could, whilst aware that moving too swiftly might appear suspicious for a priest. He didn't want anything about him to stick out in people's memories. It was as he tried to balance speed with dignity that he realised he had no idea where he was heading.

I can't just walk back into my house, it will be under watch at least. Would Orren be there, or would he be staying somewhere else? *I'll make my way to the house and walk past, see if I can figure out what's going on.*

Belasko was wary, as he moved through the crowded streets, feeling as if all eyes were on him. He tried to shake the feeling, knowing that a down-at-heel priest, as he appeared to be, would in all likelihood attract little notice. He still made sure to keep the hood of his robe pulled low. It wouldn't do for someone to spot his face. He was too well known, too easily recognised. *Which poses a question: how am I to make my way around the city, investigate the prince's poisoning, if I have to skulk and hide in the shadows?*

He turned into Founder's Way and spotted his house. He could see people milling about outside the gates. As he got closer he could make out that the small crowd was made up of city dwellers and, yes, some of the city watch. The latter were definitely parked on his doorstep, not letting anyone in or out. Belasko was aware that he had to keep on walking — stopping and turning back the way he had come would look too odd, too suspicious. He braced himself for recognition, prepared to run if necessary. *Keep your face down, just walk by. You're a priest going about your priestly business. This house is of no interest to you, and you are of no interest to those guarding it.*

As he passed by on the other side of the street, he could hear some of the crowd remonstrating with the watchmen.

"Come on, you don't think he did it, do you?"

"...no way Belasko would ever hurt the prince..."

"Poison? I mean, look, that wouldn't be his way."

The officer at the gate shook his head. "Listen," he said, then again when the crowd wouldn't quiet, "Listen!" He glared the crowd into silence. "I don't know the truth of it any more than any of you, and we're all surprised, but the Inquisition have found evidence..."

"The Inquisition? Shit on their boots!" a voice cried from the back of the crowd.

The guard continued as if he hadn't heard the interruption. "The Inquisition have found evidence and are conducting an investigation. While that investigation is carried out, we are to guard Belasko's home. That is all. I'm not going to comment on whether he's guilty or not, that's not my job — although I will admit to sadness at the thought he could be." The officer raised his voice. "Now you lot, clear off! Stop obstructing the city watch. Go on, be off with you!"

The crowd dispersed, some of them still muttering and shaking their heads. The relief that Belasko felt at the realisation that some people thought he was innocent was almost tangible. A lightening of the weight that had settled on him over the last few days.

Where to go? The house looks shut up, Orren can't be here. Then realisation came. *The Weeping Anchor. That's where he'll be.*

The Weeping Anchor was an inn in a much less salubrious part of town, that had been a haunt of theirs when they had first arrived in the city, years ago. It was the place that in those days they would always meet up at if things went sour, or they got separated. Hopefully Orren would remember that too.

But try as he might, Belasko couldn't make his way to the inn. He managed to get close, but his escape from the cells had obviously been discovered. The city watch had formed checkpoints at the gates between quarters and were inspecting and searching people as they made their way through.

His route would have to have been circuitous in any case. The city of Villan had grown around the palace over time in a series of concentric rings, and gates between quarters and through the fortified walls were not always in the most logical or accessible place. The city reflected the country as a whole, Belasko mused to himself: old, convoluted, confusing. The palace itself sat on an island in the river Lan and had been the original fortified home of the current king's distant ancestors. As their power grew, so had the settlement. The rings of the city were subdivided into various quarters, although the lines between were often a little blurry. The river that ran through the heart of the city had numerous bridges over it and sea gates that formed part of the city's network of defence. Where the river widened into an estuary that ran out to sea there were two sets of docks — one on the east side of the river, and one on the west. The western docks were for royal and naval use only, the eastern were less salubrious. It was towards the latter that Belasko was trying to get.

Damn it, so close. All Belasko had to do was get through the gate at the end of the road and he'd be in the Sea Quarter, home to the city's commercial docks, warehouses, cheap lodging houses (or brothels masquerading as such), and a number of inns and drinking dens of various levels of ill repute. The Weeping Anchor was among them. In fact, it was only a few streets away — but it may as well have been on the other side of the country. There was no way he was getting through that gate.

Maybe I don't have to.

Just ahead of him was an old sailor, distinguishable by his distinctive rolling gait, sun-darkened skin, and clothing. Baggy, loose-fitting breeches gathered in at the knee above good leather boots and a long coat taken in at the waist but flaring out below. The sailor was wearing a chain around his neck that bore the sigil of Saint Junifero, patron saint of sailors, sometimes known as the saint of the waves. One of the old pagan gods that had been brought into Aronos' retinue as a saint to encourage his worshippers to adjust their allegiance. Sailors were a superstitious lot, and if this one was returning to his ship then he wouldn't want the ill omen of refusing a request from a priest. Belasko walked up to the sailor, not needing to exaggerate his limp. "Excuse me, sir?"

The sailor turned to him, smiling to see a man of the cloth. "Hello Father, 'ow can I help ye?" He spoke with an accent that Belasko couldn't place. *Thank the gods, he's not local, less likely to recognise me.*

"I wonder, would you be able to do me a small favour and carry a message to someone for me?"

The smile on the sailor's face faltered a little. "Well Father, I'd be 'appy to 'elp, but I'm due back to my ship and the delay 'ere," he gestured at the queue of people snaking away from the gate, "well, it's already making me late."

"Oh, I see. Of course." Belasko paused. "Only, you wouldn't have to go far. It's just through the gate, actually. I just, well I injured my leg, you see, and I can't walk much further today."

The sailor frowned, looking at the gate and then back to Belasko. He sighed. "Well, if'n it's not far ..."

Belasko nodded, careful not to disturb his hood. "Thank you my son, your kindness won't be forgotten. I was due to meet an old friend, an acquaintance from the days before I joined the priesthood. I believe he's staying at the Weeping Anchor. Do you know it?"

The sailor laughed. "Afraid I do, Father. I'd say it be a good thing ye can't make it to them. The Anchor's got a poor reputation. I'm not sure ye'd want to venture inside."

Belasko smiled, shrugging. "I'm afraid I can't comment on my friend's taste in accommodation. He always kept a tight grip on his purse, which might explain it."

"He'll need to keep a tight grip on it in the Wan—Weeping Anchor.' The sailor coughed at having almost used the inn's more common nickname.

"I'm sure. Well, you'd be doing me a great favour if you were to find my friend and tell him that I'm sorry I can't make it to the inn, but that I'll be waiting at Rassan's Square, the courtyard just down that street." He pointed in the general direction. "If you could tell him that I'd be most grateful."

"How'll I know yer friend?"

"He's a tall man, big, with blond hair. Name of Orren. If you find him, tell him where I'll be."

"I will Father, and what name'll I give?"

"Oh, I think I'm the only priest he knows. Mine is an odd order, and small, you've probably not heard of it — but we give up our names when we take our vows and renounce our previous life. Just tell him his old friend, the Priest of the Blade, is waiting to meet him. He'll understand."

When he was only a street away from the square, Belasko spotted a group from the city watch. They were stopping people, asking them questions, making them throw back any raised hoods.

Oh crap. He looked around, as yet unnoticed. He spotted a

narrow alley, really only a gap between buildings, just a little further up the street. Moving quickly, but not so much as to attract attention, he darted towards it and backed in, edging away from the street.

When he stood a good few feet inside, he stopped to take in his surroundings. There wasn't much to see: some detritus had gathered at the foot of the walls to either side of him, the flotsam and jetsam of city life, but the alley contained little else. Belasko looked up at the walls that rose above him. The brickwork was old and poorly tended, mortar worn and crumbling. *Offers plenty of handholds. It's been a while since I did any climbing...*

Belasko looked up at the cliff wall stretching away above him. He reached up, found another handhold, and carried on pulling himself up. He climbed the cliff inch by inch, foot by foot. *This seemed like such a good idea this morning.*

Since the incident at Dellan Pass, he had received several field promotions and now led a small command of his own. As word spread about that day, he found it harder and harder to live up to the stories. The younger soldiers all seemed to look up to him, while the old hands gave him grudging respect. They'd been around long enough to know that nothing ever played out the way it's told around the campfire, but equally knew that he had accomplished something impressive.

Belasko and his men had gained a reputation for bold and decisive action, surprise attacks, and holding the line when it looked like things were about to go bad. He tried not to play up to this reputation, but somehow his company kept getting the dangerous jobs. The ones like this.

Earlier that day he had been called to General Garlyn's tent. The career military woman, bluff, no-nonsense, was solidly built and not softened by promotion, living as her soldiers did without recourse to the comforts her rank would have allowed. As such, she was well-liked by the soldiers under her command. She beckoned Belasko over to a map laid out on her campaign table.

"What do you think to this, Belasko? What's the best way in?"

They had been laying siege to a Baskan fort, one that was a way up in the mountains. The walls were high and the fort sat at the top of an escarpment, backing onto a perilously steep cliff.

Belasko scratched his chin. "Well ma'am, permission to speak freely?"

"Granted."

"We're not doing much good out here. We could starve them out in time, but it seems like they're well supplied and I'm not sure we have time for a prolonged waiting game."

"I agree. Go on."

"We've tried a few sorties, but have been easily rebuffed. The walls are too high and too well-fortified. We need to find a different way in."

"Yes, yes, come on."

He eyed the map for a moment, then sighed. "We go in the back."

"What, up the cliff?"

"Yes." Belasko leaned forward and tapped on the map. "This section here. The walls right at the back are low, as they're relying on the cliff to keep an attack at bay. In fact, according to the locals that were conscripted to work in its construction, they're only roughly built, almost an extension of the cliff itself, and are themselves easily climbable. I doubt they're even manned. They can't expect anyone to scale the cliff."

The general was smiling now. "You can't take a whole division of armed soldiers up there. Their armour would make the climb impossible."

Belasko shook his head. "We don't take a whole division. A small group, lightly armed, no armour to drag us down. We climb the cliff under cover of darkness, slip through the fort and open the gates. Then everyone else charges in."

"Slip through the fort, open the gates. That easy, eh? I couldn't help notice you said 'we', Belasko."

He shrugged. "Who else would you trust to do this?"

The general was grinning now. "No one. I just wanted you to figure it out for yourself before I asked you to do it." She clapped Belasko on the shoulder. "That's what I love about you Belasko, always up for something totally bloody ridiculous."

I hope the general would be happy to see that nothing's changed, Belasko thought to himself as he reached for a handhold, slowly pulling himself up the wall of the warehouse that made up one side of the alleyway. *This would have been tricky enough even if I hadn't been beaten black and blue.*

As if to prove his point, the brick of one of his handholds crumbled and his hand, suddenly free, pulled away from the wall, half swinging him out into the empty air. Pain ran through him as his whole body tensed, trying to regain control of the situation. Belasko tightened the grip of his other hand and wormed his feet more firmly into their holds. Hand scrabbling at the wall, he found another hold, a firmer one, and breathed a sigh of relief.

I really am getting too old for this.

Belasko and his soldiers, quiet as the night itself, had made their way up the cliff, slowly and carefully. Having grown up in the mountains, Belasko was an accomplished climber. He loved scaling sheer cliff faces, even as a boy. The sense of accomplishment when he reached the top of a difficult climb was like nothing else. He felt like a king when he conquered a mountain, although he had never climbed in circumstances like these.

As he and his troop neared the top, he held out his hand, palm down, gesturing to the soldiers that followed to wait.

So they waited, clinging to the cliff face, wind whistling about them, listening for any sounds from above while they rested and got their breath back. There was a distant laugh, a snatch of conversation, but nothing from directly above them. None of the sounds a guard may make — the slow exhalation of breath or the clink of armour as they shift their weight from one tired foot to another. Belasko shook his head.

He held his hand out again, turning palm down to palm up and making an upwards motion. Then he began to climb the last few feet, followed by his soldiers.

As he hauled himself onto the tile roof, gasping for breath and in pain at his injuries, other memories from that night came back to him.

He and his small force had dashed through the fort under the moon's guiding light. They moved quickly but cautiously, for they knew that if they were seen then all would be lost.

They slowed as they approached the gatehouse, ever watchful. There were guards up on the walls while the door to the gatehouse was unattended. However, the glow of lamplight through the windows indicated that someone was home.

His comrades spread out as they crossed the open ground,

coming back together outside the gatehouse. He gestured and most of them went to the gate, ready for when it opened. Orren, close by as ever, and a few others went with him to the gatehouse. The big man didn't have much of a head for heights, but ever since Dellan Pass he had stuck close to Belasko. "Look what happened when I left you to your own devices. You clearly need someone keeping an eye on you," he had said, insisting on accompanying him on the climb. He was glad of it now. He and Orren knew each other well enough that they seemed almost two sides of the same coin.

Belasko caught Orren's eye, nodding towards the door. Orren positioned himself to one side of it, checked the others were ready, then kicked it open.

Belasko was first in, the others following as quick as a flash. Belasko had his blades out, rapier and dagger, and struck quicker than thought, carving a path of destruction through the guardhouse. The occupants had obviously thought that they were settled in for a quiet night, caught as they were with feet on the table, weapons to one side, in the middle of a game of cards. They were dead before they could do more than be startled by the sudden appearance of enemy soldiers, let alone raise a cry of warning.

Belasko paused, wiping his blades on a dead man's coat as he listened for any indication that they had been heard. Satisfied that they went unnoticed, he took a lantern down from the wall, shuttering it as he pointed to the mechanism that locked the gate. "Orren, throw that. All of you, hold this building like your lives depend on it — because they do. The rest of ours too."

As Belasko went out, Orren spat on his hands. He gripped the handle of the mechanism and began to heave, muscles straining. It started to move, making a gentle clanking sound as chain and bolts withdrew. The other fighters formed up by the door, ready to repel any attackers.

Belasko crossed to his comrades stood in the gateway, nodding to the gate. They responded by setting themselves to the heavy oak and pushing. It opened, slow and ponderous, but surprisingly silent. The Baskan commander may come to regret having kept the gates so well maintained.

He opened the shutter on the lantern, closed and then opened it again. He did this several times in the prearranged signal. The gates clanged fully open and at last they were noticed.

"Here! What the bloody hell's going on?"

Belasko turned and flung the lantern at the Baskan soldier who had spoken. Its oil spilling over him, he went up in flames. Screeching, staggering, trying to put himself out, the flames lit the unfolding scene as the Baskan troops, at last alerted to the danger in their midst, converged on the gate.

Here we go again. Belasko drew his blades once more and stepped forward to the challenge.

"Come on! For Villan!" he roared, hoping to distract the enemy troops from the Villanese soldiers that were pounding over the ground between their camp and the fort. "Let's show them what we're made of!"

We showed them what some of us were made of: the same blood and guts as them, impossible to tell apart when they're spilled in the dirt.

In the now, Belasko dragged himself to his feet, gasping for breath and cursing the ache in his joints. He set off across the rooftop, feet slipping on the tiles.

He scrabbled across the intervening roofs, aware that his injuries made him clumsier than normal. He occasionally had to drop down or scramble up a few feet where the buildings that abutted each other were different heights. Eventually he reached the courtyard, peering over the lip of the roof on which he was crouched. The square wasn't empty. A small detachment of the city watch had gathered at the far side. Belasko couldn't hear what they were saying, but it looked like they were comparing notes as they consulted a map of the city. Should he wait for them to leave or find another meeting place? Belasko shook his head. *No, this is where Orren will come.* He would have to find a way down and hide from view until they were gone. Then, to his great relief, the members of the city watch concluded their discussion and, splitting into several groups, began to make their way out of the square. *Thank God for that, some good luck.* Belasko looked around, frowning. *Now, how the hell do I get down?*

6

Orren looked about him as casually as possible, as he approached the hooded figure in the square. The location was somewhat out of the way, ringed by warehouses and little-visited businesses. The dried-up well in its centre had long ago given its last and been covered over. Satisfied that there was no one else around, no one watching, he hurried up to the person in priest's robes who stood, stooped as if by age or weariness, next to the old well.

"Excuse me Father, someone said you wanted to see me? Buggered if I know any priests though..."

"You know this one well enough, old friend," the apparent priest said with a familiar voice.

"Belasko!" Orren hissed, torn between excitement and the need for stealth. The latter at least partly abandoned, he bounded up to his friend and seized him in a fierce bear hug.

Belasko hissed at the pain that flared thanks to Orren's embrace. "Alright, alright," he said, wincing as he laughed. "Gently old boy, I've been a little ill-treated of late. And perhaps less of my name in public..."

"Of course, of course." Orren released him from the hug but

kept hold of his shoulders, holding him at arms' length as he peered into the hood of Belasko's robe. He swore. "Bloody hells, what have they done to you?"

Belasko shrugged. "A little light working over, trying to get me to confess to a murder I didn't commit. Standard practice for the Inquisition, but everything should heal in time."

"Apart from that, are you alright? We need to get you out of the city."

"We'll be doing no such thing."

Orren looked stunned. "What? No, look, it's too dangerous."

"I don't care," Belasko said, struggling not to raise his voice. "Someone has set me up. For whatever reason they want me gone, to tear down everything I've built, to destroy my life and legacy. I'll be damned if I let that happen. I'm staying, and I'm going to find the real murderer. To prove myself innocent, to get some retribution for Kellan, and to show them all."

Orren looked at his friend as if he was mad. "Oh, right. And how are you to accomplish all that, then? Considering that you have to sneak around in disguises, in the shadows. The whole city is looking for you. It's said the king wants to see you hang."

Belasko shook his head. "I don't believe it. The king is grieving. Once I can prove my innocence, he'll listen to reason."

"Again, how are you going to do that?"

"Well, that's where you come in. I'm going to need a little help."

Orren was silent for a time. Then he sighed. "You know I've followed you into hopeless situations before, but this... What happens if we get caught? More importantly, what happens to Denna and my little ones? I'm not putting them in danger."

"Send them away then, we've money enough to set them up comfortably somewhere else until things have died down and it's safe for them to return."

Orren snorted. "It's you who should be spirited off to a place of safety. I know you've money lodged in other countries, enough to live comfortably where the king can never touch you."

"Don't you see?" Belasko hissed. "That's precisely what I can't do. It would be as good as an admission of guilt. No, I have to stay and prove my innocence."

"It's not just *your* innocence you need to prove."

"What?"

Orren looked around, uneasy. "The chef you found work for in the palace kitchens. The one whose dish was poisoned?"

Belasko felt the blood drain from his face. *Selfish idiot, I didn't even think about Kendra.* "Kendra. what about her? Is she well?"

"Well enough, for someone who's been locked up since the prince was killed."

"Have they...?"

"Beaten her, like they did you?" Orren shrugged. "I don't think so. They're letting her send notes to her father. Apparently she's being treated well enough. An inquisitor — Ervan, I think — has even let her have a few creature comforts."

"Do they think she poisoned the prince?"

"No, it seems like the blame for that is being laid solely on your head. I get the feeling that they can't quite work out what to do with her. Either that or they're holding on to her just in case. In case of what, I don't know."

Belasko released a breath he didn't know he'd been holding. "I didn't even think. Damn it. I've got to do this for her, too. We've both been set up, and she's been used to get to me. I'm sure of it. What to do?"

Orren sighed. "The first thing I'm doing is getting my wife and children out of harm's way. They can go and visit her family in Annor until this all blows over. Then we need to find you somewhere to stay. A safe-house. Do you have any friends, other than me, who aren't out for your blood?"

~

Lilliana looked at the scene before her: the dark-haired young woman dozing in her chair, the book she had been reading fallen open on her lap. It was quite a peaceful scene, its normality offset by its location in one of the palace cells. A brazier glowed in the corner, giving off some heat in a vain attempt to beat back the cold and damp of the dungeons.

"Belasko's living quarters were not quite so nice, I think."

Her voice startled the young woman awake and she leapt to her feet. When she saw her visitor she gawped for a moment before flushing and dropping into a hurried curtsy, dropping her book in the process.

"Oh, don't do that on my account. But please, pick up your book. I'm sure the cell floor is no place to be keeping reading material."

Kendra flushed an even deeper red before grabbing up her book and holding it to her chest. "I'm sorry, your highness."

Lilliana smiled. "I'm only joking. What is it you're reading?"

Kendra returned her smile, red face subsiding a little. "It's a simple thing, a collection of stories my father used to read me when I was little. I just wanted a reminder of home, considering..." She looked around her and sighed.

"I quite understand." Lilliana nodded. "Although I have to say you are being treated better than Belasko — before he escaped, that is."

Kendra blinked at the princess. "Belasko... escaped? I hadn't... I hadn't realised."

"Oh yes, earlier today. The whole city is in an uproar. The city watch are teeming through the streets trying to find him. It's all quite exciting."

"But if he ran, I mean, maybe that means..." Kendra looked crestfallen. Then she shook her head. "No, I'm sure of him."

"Sure of him how?"

Kendra flushed again. "I'm sorry your highness, for your loss. I only met your brother once and he was kind to me. I know what it is to lose a loved one, and you have my utmost sympathy. It's just I can't believe Belasko had anything to do with it." There was a long silence which dragged on uncomfortably, until eventually Kendra broke it. "I'm sorry highness, I spoke out of turn. I—"

"You are quite right. I agree with you. There's no way anyone who actually knows Belasko would think him capable of killing my brother. There's something very rotten going on here, if only I could figure out what." Lilliana paused, tapping her fingers on her chin, bright eyes squinting at Kendra in thought. "Do you, perhaps, know anything?"

"I've already told the inquisitor everything I know," Kendra said. "There were several visitors to the kitchen that day, but Belasko was one of the only people, other than myself, to go near my workstation while I was preparing dessert for the prince. I—"

"Wait. You said 'one of' — there were others?"

Kendra nodded. "Yes. Inquisitor Ervan came to the kitchens to ask me a few questions. He said they were normal procedure when hiring someone for the palace staff. As I returned to work, I saw someone walking away from my workstation."

"Who?"

Kendra swallowed. "One of the other kitchen workers, a young man called Tarvin. I mentioned it to the inquisitor and he said that Tarvin had been planning to put something in the food as a prank, but he'd questioned him and apparently the presence of an inquisitor put him off going through with it. I mean, Tarvin is an arse, but—"

"And the inquisitor, Ervan, who just happens to be leading the investigation into my brother's murder, came to visit you to ask you questions, taking you away from your workstation long enough that this Tarvin *could* have put something in the food?"

"Um, yes. That's right."

Lilliana nodded. "Interesting. You said there were several visitors to the kitchens. Who else came there that day?"

"There was a member of the Baskan ambassador's staff. A jumped up little man, supposed to be bringing instructions for a Baskan dish that was to be served at a reception. He toured the kitchens, criticising everything. But I was working the entire time he was in the kitchen, I'm sure he didn't come near enough to have done anything." For a moment Kendra looked uncertain. "At least, I think so. I've been over the events of that day so many times in my head, I'm beginning to doubt myself."

Lilliana was quiet for a moment, tapping her fingers on her chin as she thought. "You know, it seems strange to me for an inquisitor of Ervan's rank to interview new staff. I'm sure those sorts of enquiries should be made before you even walk through the palace gates. His presence, the Baskan ambassador's staff... I have questions and I'm unsure how to go about getting answers." She looked at Kendra for a moment. "I've got to go. People will get suspicious if I spend much more time down in the cells. But I'll be back to visit you again. I can't say when exactly, but I'll slip away when I can. I'll have some more reading material sent down to you."

"Thank you Princess Lilliana, that's very kind."

Lilliana snorted in a most unladylike fashion. "I don't know about 'kind'. It's the least I can do for someone who seems to have been used as a pawn in the murder of my only brother. That sort of thing makes me angry. Very angry."

Kendra met her eyes. "Me too, your highness. Me too."

"Come." Ambassador Aveyard called, replying to the knock on her study door. Although the ambassador's residence was suitably sumptuous in its decor and furnishings, this room reflected the military officer she had once been. That, in her own mind, she still was. It was plain, minimally furnished, practical. Orderly, except for the stacks of paperwork on her desk that always seemed to remain the same size. No matter how much of it she dealt with, her secretary always managed to find more work for her. She looked up from the letter she was writing as the door opened to admit that secretary, Jonteer, a thin man with an impassive face and fringe of greying hair encircling his balding head, his olive Baskan complexion made sallow by years in Villan's colder climate. *What secrets lurk beneath that hairless dome?* the ambassador thought to herself, although she harboured enough of her own. While Jonteer worked for her, she didn't doubt that he reported back to his true employers, the Baskan Intelligence Service.

Jonteer approached her desk and stood silent, waiting for her request or command.

"Well?" she asked. "Any word on Belasko?"

Her secretary shook his head. "No my lady, nothing yet, but we are keeping our eyes and ears open. It has only been a few hours. If we hear of anything, you will be the first to know."

She snorted. "Yes, but only because it will take time for your other messages to travel home."

The small smile he gave her did not touch his eyes. "My first duty is to our homeland, as you know, but I am ever your obedient servant."

Aveyard waved her hand, indicating that Jonteer should sit down. He took the seat opposite her. "I know, I know. You are a most able secretary and, more importantly, intelligence gatherer. How do you think Belasko did it? I saw his cell. Escape should have been impossible."

Jonteer nodded. "You're quite right. The only conceivable way he could have escaped is with help from inside the palace. A friendly guard perhaps, or court functionary. However he did it, nobody's talking. The palace has sealed itself up tight and is keeping a firm hold on any information they have. Perhaps it's too little too late, but I'm sure we'll soon discover something. In the meantime, I'll task our operatives to keep an eye out and report back if they find anything."

The ambassador sat back in her chair, drumming the fingers of one hand on her desk. "What do you think, Jonteer? Did he do it?" Her secretary shrugged, face impassive. "Did *we* do it?" If anything his face stilled even further at this question. "If we had, would I even be told? Or would I be kept out of the loop to lend my denial plausibility?"

"I couldn't possibly say, madam Ambassador. That sort of thinking is far beyond my humble station."

She frowned. "If we did do it — and I'm not saying that we did — then I have to say that the thinking escapes me. Prince Kellan was harmless, with plenty of weaknesses that we could have exploited to our advantage. Taking him off the table only confuses the game. Unless something else is planned, to destabilise the situation further? Bah, this circular thinking will get me nowhere. Plots within plots. You see what this sort of politicking has done to me? I miss the days of honest, straightforward warfare. Peace doesn't suit me."

Jonteer said nothing. She leaned forward, elbows on her desk. "Tell me, have you got any further with infiltrating the city's underworld? That might be a good source of information."

"No, my lady, to my regret we have not." Now it was Jonteer's turn to frown. "We have connections with the outer circles but haven't been able to penetrate further. I feel as though there is a shadowy figure at the centre of it all, controlling the web as it were, but if so then they play the game very well."

"A 'shadowy figure'?" Aveyard laughed. "Not this Water King that the Villanese people use to frighten their children? Maybe I should try that on you. Be a good little secretary or the Water King will come at night and eat your feet!"

Jonteer gave her a dry smile. "Very droll, my lady. No, not a fictional monster, but..." He shook his head. "Definitely someone, and it pains me that I'm unable to find out more. I will keep trying. As you say, the criminal element of the city could be quite useful. I will advise you if anything comes up. Do I have your permission to withdraw and attend to my duties?"

Aveyard nodded. "Yes, of course. I have my own work to attend to. These letters won't write themselves." She tapped a stack of paperwork on her desk.

Jonteer stood, pushing back his chair before replacing it neatly with his usual economy of movement. He collected a pile of the ambassador's finished work and went to the door, saluting the ambassador before he went out. Aveyard returned his salute almost lazily.

Jonteer paused, one hand on the door handle, before turning back to face the ambassador. "There is one more thing, Ambassador."

"Yes, Jonteer?"

He coughed, looking slightly embarrassed. "The Inquisition have requested a meeting. A member of the ambassadorial staff was present in the kitchens the night the prince was poisoned. They'd like to discuss that with you."

Aveyard sat up in her seat. "A member of staff? Who? Why?"

At this Jonteer looked positively shamefaced. "It was I, Ambassador. You asked me to discuss some of the preparations for the dinner that was supposed to take place this evening, do you remember? I merely visited the kitchens to make sure everything would be suitably arranged. The dinner has been postponed in any event, but the timing is awkward."

Aveyard looked at him for a moment, a feeling of cold uncertainty opening up in her belly. "Yes. Yes it is. Schedule them into the diary at once. I'll entertain them here. I've no desire to see the inside of a Villanese cell from the wrong side of the bars." Jonteer nodded and was about to leave when she spoke again. "Actually Jonteer, there is another thing you could do for me."

"Yes, madam Ambassador?"

"If we do hear anything about Belasko and are in a position to act, I would be inclined to see if we can capture him ourselves. Or at least entice him to come to us."

"Forgive me my lady, but why?" Jonteer's always inscrutable face was now completely expressionless.

"He's too powerful a player in these events to have him running about on his own. If we control him, we control the flow of events. We may be able to use that to our advantage, to distract the king, or curry favour. I'm having a difficult time convincing him the incidents along our border aren't officially sanctioned and it's only a matter of time before the current drama ceases to hold all of his attention. But tread delicately. Our presence here is a tentative step towards reparations between our people. It wouldn't do for us to be caught meddling in such sensitive matters."

"Very good, madam." With that Jonteer let himself out, leaving Ambassador Aveyard to her work.

She stared at the door for a long moment after he had gone. *It's coincidence that he was in the kitchens, nothing more, I'm sure. At least, I hope.* She shook her head and looked at the piles of paperwork before her. She sighed. "Damn, but I need a brandy," she proclaimed to the empty room.

Lilliana moved through the corridors of the palace, flanked by a pair of guards. She stopped at a set of double doors and turned to them. "Do you really have to follow me so closely? Please don't take offence, but it's becoming quite annoying."

The guards, a little shamefaced, exchanged looks. One stood to attention and said, "I'm sorry your highness, it's the king's orders. You are not to be left unattended. He's very concerned for your safety."

"I'm sure, I'm sure, but I'm just going into the palace library." She gestured at the doors before them. "I want to look something up and I may be a while. There's only this entrance, and my father's private study is just down the corridor. He'll almost certainly be in there now with his own guards. Why don't you just wait outside the door? I get some privacy and you don't have to watch me poring over musty old books. How does that sound?"

The guards exchanged looks once again. The one who had spoken previously said, "I think that would be alright, if we check the room first. Make sure it's empty and there are no other ways in."

Lilliana smiled. "Excellent! Let's get on with it, then I can concentrate on my studies." She gestured again towards the door. "Go on, in you go."

The guards opened the doors and peered into the room. A high-ceilinged room, dust danced in the light that fell from tall windows onto shelves stacked with books. In fact, books were everywhere. On the towering shelves, open or piled up on desks placed around the room, filling the cupboards that lined the walls. The guards made their way inside, followed by the princess. She started collecting the books she needed and moved them onto a desk set against the wall opposite the entrance. The guards checked under the furniture, opening the cupboards and inspecting every possible hiding place. Eventually they came to her desk and stood to attention.

"Everything alright?" she asked. "No one lurking in the corners?"

"No, ma'am," said the first guard. "All clear."

"Would you like us to leave you now, your highness?" asked the second. "We'll bar anyone from entering while you're in here."

Lilliana smiled. "That sounds delightful. I should bring you along every time I use the library, to guarantee some peace and quiet."

"Alright," said the second guard. "We'll be right outside. Call if you need anything."

"Thank you gentlemen, most kind."

The guards saluted, clicked their heels, and left the library in their best parade ground march. The door shut behind them.

Lilliana sighed. *Alone at last.* She almost never had time alone anymore, felt that she was being watched constantly. She bent her head over the books open in front of her and started to read.

As she worked her way through her reading material, she became aware of a faint sound. Lilliana frowned. It sounded like the murmur of distant voices. She looked around, a smile working its way across her face as her eyes alighted on a cupboard built into the wall that the library shared with her father's study. She moved over to the cupboard, kneeling in front of it as she opened its doors. *I'd almost forgotten about you. My old hiding place.*

It was a place she had found years ago, while playing some childish game with Kellan. A cupboard, tucked away in the corner of the palace library. Later she would come and hide there whenever she wanted some peace and quiet, or just her own company, in the difficult years after her mother died.

The cupboard was curious in its construction. The palace library and her father's private study had been connected in the past, joined by a door that this cupboard, and a matching one on the other side, had been built to replace when King Mallor had felt a need for more privacy some years prior. If you were to climb inside it, as a small child might, you could at times hear what was said in the next room quite clearly.

Although it was big enough that Lilliana had easily been

able to climb inside when she was a child, that would prove impossible now. Not just because she had grown, but because her clothes restricted her movements. Gone were the simple robes she had worn as a child, and although she wasn't currently clad in a formal gown, even the informal dresses she wore in the royal quarters had layers of skirts and some corsetry.

I wonder...

Lilliana knelt in front of the cupboard with some difficulty, skirts bunched around her, and put her head inside . As she closed her eyes darkness enveloped her, along with a familiar mustiness that she hadn't smelled in years. She smiled to herself. The sounds were clearer now. If she listened closely she could make out the conversation from next door.

7

A group of city watch came into the square from the opposite side. "Damn it," said Orren, "you'll have to make yourself scarce. I'll distract them while you slip away."

"Don't do anything foolish."

The big man snorted. "I'm only going to talk to them. We don't all have your flair for the dramatic. Oh, I've an idea."

"What's that?" Belasko was trying to keep Orren between himself and the approaching city watch.

"Lord Hibberth, do you remember him?"

"Yes, although I haven't seen him in a while — not since that thing with the jugglers at the Countess D'aviland's party."

"He's a good man, and a friend of mine to boot. Go to him. He'll give you a bed for the night at least. He owes me a favour." Orren turned towards the city watch and spread his arms wide. "Gentlemen! Isn't it a glorious day? Just when we are all low with grief, Aronos above sends us a day like this! Now, you look like men about some business. How can I assist you?"

Orren's voice faded as Belasko withdrew into the shadows at the edge of the square. By keeping the bigger man between himself and the watch, he was able to move without being noticed. He edged into a road that led away from the square and picked up the pace.

~

The sky was just beginning to darken as Belasko made his way to Lord Hibberth's door. The journey had taken him some time via his quite roundabout route, having to double back on himself multiple times to avoid the watch. Another rooftop escapade, a dash through a slaughterhouse, a brief sojourn through the sewers that served the more illustrious parts of the city. *Everyone else is content to throw their shit in the streets. Only the wealthy get it carried away for them.*

He didn't bother with the front door, but went straight to the servants' entrance. He knocked, and when no answer came, knocked again.

This time he could hear someone clumping towards the door, which opened to reveal a pinch-faced old man whose countenance relaxed when he saw Belasko's pilfered priest's robes.

"Hello Father, how can I be of assistance?"

"Sorry to bother you so late," Belasko said, assuming the tones of an older man, "but I bear a message for your master. Would it be possible to deliver it in person?"

The servant's face regained a little of its stiffness. "Well, it is most irregular ..."

"I know good sir, but I only need a little of his time. It is to pass on the word of one Orren Osberson, who asked me to bring this message as he knew I was passing nearby."

The servant sniffed. "The name is not unknown to me. Will you come in and warm yourself by the fire? I'll ask his lordship if he'll see you."

Belasko shuffled in and was shown through the scullery into the kitchen and on into the main part of the house. The kitchen led on to a large dining room via a discrete serving door. The master of the house clearly liked to entertain and this room was opulent and lavishly appointed. The furniture was polished to a rosy glow, seats laden with cushions, and it seemed every surface gleamed with mother of pearl inlay or gold leaf. Belasko was shown through another door into a small lounge which was a little more modest in its décor if no less comfortable. A cosy fireplace even contained a small fire. He was thankful for small mercies. He crouched by the fire, hoping the heat would ease his aching joints. After a while he stood, still holding his hands to the flames. The door opened with a slight rattle.

"Alright, what's this all about? I'm surprised Orren would send a priest to collect his gambling debts, but to each his own."

Belasko turned to see Lord Hibberth as he came into the room. A short and stout man of middle years, his eyes normally held a mischievous twinkle and now gleamed with curiosity.

"No my lord, it is not about gambling debts," Belasko said, still in the voice he had used at the door. "Although this night might prove a gamble for us both. Would you mind closing the door? I'm rather enjoying the warmth of the fire and it's letting the heat out."

"Of course, bear with me." Hibberth came into the room, closing the door soundly behind him. "Now what is this about? What does Orren have to say that is so urgent?" The lord made his way over to Belasko as he spoke.

Belasko, returning to his normal voice, said, "Orren wishes you to know that his friend, Belasko the swordsman, is not guilty of the murder of Prince Kellan." He took a deep breath then stood up straight, pulling back his hood as he did so. "I wish you to know this, too."

He knew revealing his identity was a risk, but Belasko was short of allies and needed all the help he could get. Besides, he was confident he could overpower the little lord and his retinue and escape, if it came to that.

Lord Hibberth gawped at Belasko, eyes boggling, before looking around frantically as if he expected the room to be suddenly full of people. Then he closed on Belasko, seizing his arm roughly as he peered at the duellist's bruised and battered face. "Belasko," he hissed, "what have they done to you?" He shook his head. "And what are you doing here? Are you trying to get me hanged along with yourself?"

Belasko shook his head. "No my lord, the very opposite. I'm trying to prove my innocence. I just need somewhere to stay tonight, to avoid notice while I figure things out. Orren suggested I come to you."

"He did, did he?" Hibberth sighed. "Well he can consider my debt wiped clean after this. Now, please sit. Let us draw some chairs closer to the fire and I'll send for some tea. You have to tell me everything, and we'll see how I can help you. Do raise your hood while I talk to the servants, it'll be no good if you get recognised now."

Some time later, after several cups of tea had been drunk, Hibberth sat back and folded his hands over his belly. He regarded Belasko with a watchful eye, then got up to stoke the fire. "Well," he said, stabbing at the logs with the poker, "it really is remarkable. You manage to go from," stab, stab, "king's favourite," stab, stab, "to enemy of the people overnight." Stab, stab. He replaced the poker in its stand and turned back to Belasko. "I have to say, it does all seem rather fishy. And obvious, to any who know you or our late lamented prince, that it is very unlikely that you would kill him. For that reason, I accept your protestations of innocence. If I help you, I hope you'll forgive my debt to you. From that thing, that time with the jugglers."

Belasko breathed a sigh of relief. "Thank you, my lord. Now I just need to prove it to the king."

"Yes, well, that is a fight for another day. Although it is most odd that he... never mind. Something to discuss by the fresh light of day. Let me think tonight on what help I might give you. Is there anyone else we can turn to for assistance?"

Belasko shook his head. "I don't know. Any authority and connections I have are mostly a result of my closeness to the throne. Now..." He spread his hands wide. "I just don't know."

Hibberth barked a humourless laugh, a sour expression on his face. "You might as well go down to the docks, find some dark place in the dead of night and summon the Water King. He'll know who poisoned the prince. They say there's not a thing goes on in the city, not a pocket picked, a house burgled, that he doesn't have an involvement with."

"They also say he's ten foot tall and half-man, half-sea monster. While I've seen some things in my time... city life shelters you from certain realities. But while there are creatures out on the fringes of our country that would make your hair curl, I think I'll have to make do without assistance from fictitious criminal beasts."

Hibberth sighed. "Well then, we'll have to figure it out on our own. You go to bed now. Rest and try to recuperate from your ordeal."

"Thank you. I didn't realise how tired I was until I sat down." Belasko felt the truth of his words as a great wave of exhaustion washed over him. He yawned. "In fact, I'm not sure how I'm still conscious."

"Me neither. I'll have you taken up to one of the guest rooms so you can get some sleep. Back on with the hood — no need to scare the servants." Hibberth rose and went to the door.

He opened it and called for a servant while Belasko pulled up his hood. Within moments Hibberth's servant reappeared.

"The good Father will be staying with us this evening, it's far too late to send him back out into the dark. Would you be so kind as to show him up to one of the guest rooms? I believe the blue suite is made up?" The servant nodded and stood to one side, waiting for Belasko, who heaved himself up from his chair with a groan. Hibberth turned to him and beckoned him over. "Here Father, go with Meerling. He'll see you settled for the night."

And so it was that, for the first time in what felt like an eternity, Belasko slept in a comfortable bed. Sleep rose up and claimed him as soon as his head hit the pillow and, for once, he fell into a deep and dreamless sleep.

Sadly his sleep was rudely interrupted when he was shaken awake by Lord Hibberth early the following morning. Belasko blinked, then tried to clear the sleep from his eyes with the back of his hand. "Alright, alright! What's the matter?"

"You have to get up, now." The stout little lord was red-faced and sweating.

"Whatever's the matter, my lord? You're positively shaking."

"Quickly, quickly, up! The inquisitors' men are here. Well, not here, but it's only a matter of time. They're going house to house and insisting on searching for an escapee from the palace cells. They don't mention you by name, but it can't be anyone else."

"Damn it," Belasko said as he bolted out of bed, "I can't believe the nobility are standing for that."

"I don't think they have much choice, although they will all be grumbling up their sleeves about it. There's not much time, but come into the next room. I've a few things that might help you."

Belasko pulled on his hose and shirt as quickly as he could before grabbing his doublet. He made a face at the smell that came back from his clothes. *Too many days in a cell without a bath. I can't be any better.*

Lord Hibberth turned back to him and saw the look on Belasko's face. He sighed. "Yes, I'm sorry we haven't had time to launder your clothes or draw you a bath, but it will help with the disguise I've put together for you."

Belasko followed Hibberth into the next room. "Disguise?"

The little lord gestured to a table on which he had laid out several items. "A relic of my younger days, when I caused quite the scandal by running off and joining a mummer's troupe for the summer. I've had a penchant for dressing up ever since. These are for you."

Belasko took in the items, which included a stained and tattered hooded robe, much less fine than his priest's garments, a gnarled walking stick, and several pots of greasepaint.

"Perhaps fitting for your current situation, we are going to turn you into a diseased beggar that even the stoutest Inquisitor will balk at inspecting. Now come over to this mirror so I can give you some sores. Pay attention, you'll have to reapply these paints every so often."

A few minutes later, as members of the Inquisition knocked on the front door, Belasko was ushered out the back of the house.

"Here," said Hibberth as he thrust a jingling purse into Belasko's hands. "It's all I could scrape together at a moment's notice, but it should be enough to get you through a few days."

"Thank you, for everything," Belasko said, as he tucked the purse into the ratty cloth bag that Hibberth had given him in place of the priest's satchel.

"Don't thank me yet. I'll try to stall them at the door as long as I can. Get as far away from here as you can. Wait for things to die down a little, then perhaps we can put a roof over your head again." The sounds of banging on the front door came over Hibberth's shoulder. He sighed. "Those brutes will mark the paint! Right, off with you, and fare you well." With no further ado he turned and closed the door firmly behind him, and Belasko set off.

He had only just turned the corner of the alley that ran behind Lord Hibberth's house when he heard shouts. A man and woman in the black jackets and hose of the Inquisition stood at the mouth of the alleyway. The man gestured imperiously. "You there, come here. Come here at once."

Belasko walked slowly up to them, leaning heavily on his walking stick and affecting a limp. *Not much of an affectation at the moment.* He put on a wheedling tone to his voice as he spoke. "Sorry m'lords, what's the trouble?"

Their noses wrinkling in disgust at the fake lesions and sores that Hibberth had applied to his arms, the inquisitors looked at each other. The man that had called him over spoke, disgust apparent in his voice. "We're looking for someone. A dangerous man. He escaped from the cells at the palace and we're tasked with searching the city until we find him."

Belasko gave a hacking cough, before turning to spit on the ground behind him. "Sorry, m'lords. I wouldn't know anything about that. I was just sleeping in this alley here last night, trying to stay out of the way. Didn't see no men, dangerous or not. I'd tell you if I had."

"I'm sure you would. Just do us a favour and throw back your hood a moment. Then you can be about your... business."

"My hood? I'm not sure you'd like what you see sir, I keep it pulled down for a reason."

"The sooner you show us your face, the sooner you can be off and we can move on."

"Alright m'lord, if you're sure." Belasko raised hesitant

hands up to his face, one of them still clutching the walking stick. Quick as a flash he lashed out, clipping the male inquisitor to his left on the chin with the handle of the walking stick. As his eyes rolled back, stunned, Belasko thrust the other end of the walking stick into the female inquisitor's stomach. As the second inquisitor doubled over in pain, Belasko turned on his heel and ran as fast as he could.

For the rest of that day, Belasko moved through the city. His disguise rendered him invisible to most, who would rather ignore a beggar than admit there was a problem with vagrancy in the city. He was on the receiving end of a few kicks from guards when he found himself too close to a lord or lady in the crowded streets, and was spat at more than once, but other than that he seemed free to wander the city as he wished. As long as he stayed a few steps ahead of wherever the Inquisition were searching. He stayed within the same quarter, not wanting to risk the searches that were still being conducted at the gates into other parts of the city. This slowed his progress and the streets were snarled with bored and irritated people just trying to go about their business.

There was an odd atmosphere on the streets, a mix of fear and mourning. Many people wore a patch of black about their person, or black ribbons in their hair, in honour of their fallen prince, and there seemed a dullness to many people's expressions.

The kings, princes and princesses of this world, the lords and ladies, those above us — they're supposed to be safe, their expressions seemed to say. *If they're not, what about the rest of us? If the prince can be killed in his own palace, surrounded by guards, how can they keep the rest of us safe?*

These thoughts and more also ran through Belasko's mind

as he tried to make sense of what had happened. He frowned, shaking his head as he rested for a moment in the mouth of an alley.

As he rested he began to listen to the world around him, the people that passed by, the snippets of conversation that could be overheard.

A pair of matronly older women walked by, one as tall and thin as the other was short and round. The tall woman sniffed, saying to the other, "It's a shame about the prince. Although you used to hear all sorts of things about what he got up to..."

The shorter woman shook her head, saying, "True, true, but he'd have grown out of that. Given time."

Two workmen passed the other way, carrying heavy timber over their shoulders. The one leading called back to his fellow, "I know he used to drink a fair bit, mess about with women and all that, but he seemed like a good bloke to me. Underneath it all."

The workman bringing up the rear grunted as he shifted the heavy timber. "Met him often, did you? Always playing cards with him down the tavern, I bet."

A young couple followed in the footsteps of the older ladies, arm in arm, talking quietly. Both seemed sad. The young man pushed back slightly too long hair with his free hand. "It's a shame," he said, "that we won't get to see what sort of a king he would have made."

The young woman squeezed his hand and said, "I'm sure he would have been better than many expected. The apple doesn't fall that far from the tree. I'm sure he took after his father in his better qualities."

Belasko smiled as a young mother walked in the other direction, dragging a complaining child behind her by the hand. "Now you stop your whining and behave, or I'll take you down to the docks and leave you for the Water King. He'll gobble you up in no time at all! They say naughty children are his favourite food."

Belasko frowned in the depths of his hood. So what if Kellan had a bit of a bad reputation? He was still loved. He shook his head. There was also the nature of his murder to be considered. Poison was not cheap, and for it to be so effectively targeted and not indiscriminate — foreign agents, perhaps? Hidden in the kitchen or serving staff? Never mind what the Baskan ambassador said in Belasko's cell, they were as likely to be behind this as anyone. It could all be politically motivated. Change the succession, plunge the nation into mourning... but Lilliana was more than capable as heir, some would say better suited to the role then Kellan. So who would profit from this?

Around and around such thoughts ran, as he approached the house of a friend. He had tried two others that day, people he was sure would listen to him and provide a roof, even for only one night, but he had been rebuffed. Not by his friends, but by their staff, for their masters were not at home. It seemed that being an associate of Belasko's was currently a dangerous occupation and several of his acquaintances had absented themselves from the city. Although in both cases their staff had taken pity on a poor beggar and found him some scraps to eat, so it wasn't a total loss.

Which was why he found himself approaching this particular door, gnawing on a heel of bread. *A bit of a gamble, but I think it will pay off.*

The house he approached was more humble than some of the others he had visited that day, for it belonged to only a minor member of the nobility and was situated on the very edge of the quarter, where descending nobility met the upwardly mobile and had to rub along together. A former army officer, he and Belasko had been friends since their service in the Last War. More importantly, he had also been a friend of Prince Kellan's. One of his inner circle and a regular drinking companion, he was unlikely to have left the city. He also had few staff, which meant he might open the door himself and Belasko was more likely to gain entrance.

Belasko readied himself, then reached for the door knocker.

The man who opened it was tall, with dark hair speckled with grey at the temples, and he peered down at Belasko. He frowned to find an apparent beggar on his doorstep before looking around, perhaps to see if this was some sort of prank.

"Yes? Can I help you?"

Belasko reached up and drew back his hood. The man's eyes widened in surprise, his face paled in shock. "I hope to hell you can Osric, otherwise I've no friends left."

Osric looked around again before grabbing Belasko by the shoulder and pulling him into the house, closing the door firmly behind them. Once they were inside he held Belasko at arms' length, staring at him, face still pale with shock.

"Well, go on, say something," said Belasko. "You're starting to make me nervous."

Osric laughed, a sour note to his voice. "You, nervous? You've ice for blood if you're walking around the city. They say... they say you poisoned Prince Kellan."

"Who says that, Osric? Who? You and I both know it's nonsense. I loved Kellan. I may have given him a few bruises on the training ground, but other than that I'd never harm him."

Osric nodded, letting go of Belasko. "I know, I know. It was the Inquisition. They paid me a visit yesterday, said I was to let them know if you visited."

Belasko felt his blood run cold. "And will you?"

Osric snorted. "No, of course not. Come in. We need to get you a bath and some clean clothes by the smell of it. Then you'll tell me everything."

"Thank you. The cells at the palace are not known for their bathing facilities."

"Well, it's the maid's day off, so we'll have to get you sorted ourselves. But I'd wager I still provide more comfort than a prison cell." As they moved down the hallway, Osric stopped and turned again to Belasko. "But if you didn't kill Prince Kellan, who did?"

Belasko met his eyes with a look of steely determination. "I don't know, but I intend to find out."

8

That night, freshly bathed and with some borrowed clothes laid out for the morning, Belasko slept once again in a comfortable bed.

He and Osric had sat up half the night, going over what they knew of the prince's death, around and around in circles as they tried to figure out just who might have wanted Kellan dead badly enough to have acted on it. A dozen jilted lovers and insulted courtiers were dismissed as having neither the resources or capacity to have carried out the poisoning, and they were left in the same position in which they had started. They didn't know who had killed Prince Kellan, just that it wasn't Belasko.

As they sat and talked, tiredness affected them both differently. Belasko's weariness was bone deep, slowing him down. If anything, Osric seemed to get more twitchy and restless as the evening wore on.

"I don't understand," Osric said as they sipped wine by his fireplace, picking aimlessly at the arm of his chair. "Why frame you? Why not just have the prince poisoned and leave it as a mystery?"

"Well," Belasko mused, "this way they avoid further investigation. As there's a ready-made fool to take the blame, there's no need to look into things further. Plus, if they hadn't implicated me then I would be amongst the people leading the investigation. Perhaps they feared my involvement? I don't know. None of it makes sense. I just feel that if I could take a step back, get a wider view of events, maybe then something would present itself."

"Tricky to do while you're on the run and the Inquisition comb the streets for you. Still, at least you can rest easy here tonight. The Inquisition already paid me a visit. I doubt they'll be back in the next day or so."

"Thank you, Osric. It's good to know that you believe me." Belasko blinked, head suddenly heavier than before. Osric smiled at him, eyes red from tiredness and a surfeit of wine.

"That I do. Looks like you'd best be off up to bed. Your head is nodding."

"I'll not disagree. I think you'd best get some rest too, my friend. Goodnight, Osric."

"Goodnight, Belasko."

Belasko was startled awake when the door to his bedroom crashed open. He tried to get up, but his limbs felt heavy. His head felt heavy too, as if it was too big for his neck.

Two big men in black came through the door, followed by a familiar one-eyed figure. "Hello Belasko, good to see you again," said Ervan with a cold smile.

The other two men grabbed Belasko and dragged him out of bed in his smallclothes while he feebly tried to resist.

"Having a bit of a struggle this morning, are we? Sorry about that. We gave Osric something to put in your wine, should you pay a visit. A little something to knock you out and make you a bit more tractable this morning. We hardly wanted to face you at full strength."

As Belasko struggled with the men at the top of the stairs, he could see a tall figure further along the corridor. Osric looked on, pale with a mournful expression on his face.

"Why?" Belasko mumbled, stricken at his friend's betrayal.

Osric flinched. "I'm sorry Belasko, truly. When they visited me before, they told me that if you came by I had to tell them. It's..." The tall man looked down at his feet. "Awndle powder," he whispered. "I'm addicted. They threatened to tell my sister. Tell her everything. She controls the family estates. If she knew, she'd cut me off." Osric looked up to Belasko with a stricken expression on his face and tears in his eyes. "What could I do? What could I do?"

Belasko could see it now. The eyes he thought were wide in surprise at his arrival were staring. The paleness he had noted the previous night was an unhealthy pallor. The signs were there but he was so wrapped up in his own situation he hadn't noticed the tell-tale signs in his friend that were common in users of the powerful narcotic.

As the two men holding him pulled a sack over his head and dragged him down the stairs, Belasko could hear Osric calling after them, "Don't hurt him! He's innocent. You said you wouldn't hurt him!"

Belasko was taken into the street and thrown onto something hard, wooden. *A wagon?* he wondered. Then he was struck on the back of the head and lost consciousness.

When Belasko came to, he was pretty sure he was still lying where he had been thrown, still being taken wherever it was that Ervan wished him to go. The jerking, bumpy motion confirmed his final thought that he was riding on the back of a wagon. He tried to move but found that his hands and feet were tightly bound. He froze as a hand patted him on the shoulder, followed by the inquisitor's voice.

"Don't struggle Belasko, you'll only hurt yourself. Save your strength. You'll need it."

Belasko quieted, trying to take in the sounds of his surroundings, but he could hear little above the creaking rattle of the wagon.

Are those gulls? Belasko was sure he could hear the high, thin cry of the birds. *Perhaps the docks.* It wasn't a reassuring thought — the city docks were an easy place to dispose of a body. The rising smell of sour salt water and the detritus that always gathers where populated land meets the sea only confirmed his suspicions.

Eventually they came to a jolting halt and Belasko could just make out a low murmur of conversation. The wagon bed lurched as people got off and then strong hands seized the ropes at his ankles and wrists, and he was dragged off the wagon. Then he was grabbed by the arms and lifted. The sound of boots on cobbles was replaced by boots on planks and then floorboards. He was placed on a chair and the ropes at his ankles and wrists removed. His hands were put behind the back of the chair and the ropes retied, pulled through a hook fixed to the back of the chair that he could just feel with his fingertips.

Then the sounds of footsteps moving away, a door slammed shut, and silence. Belasko sat still, listening to his own breathing. Faintly, he could make out someone else's intake of breath.

Not alone after all.

Slowly, trying not to let his body give the movement away, Belasko splayed his hands behind his back, trying to feel along the ropes that held him. They searched for a weak point, a sharp surface, anything that might help him free himself from his bonds. His questing fingers explored the hook. *There.* The tip of the hook was sharp. *That might do it...*

He waited, not knowing how many others were in the room and not wanting to give away his plan to anyone stood behind him. Again, he heard the sound of another's breath, then the dull clank of something being put on a table in front of him. Belasko could feel the presence of someone stood close to him, then the sack was pulled from his head and he blinked against the sudden light.

Ervan stood back, watching him for a moment, before taking a seat across from Belasko behind a table that was positioned between them. As his vision cleared, Belasko could see what lay before him on the table. A rapier, of the sort he favoured for duelling. Ignoring the inquisitor for the moment, he craned his neck around, trying to see if there was anyone else in the room. It was bare of almost all features, the floorboards old and splintering, and had the air of a place long unused. There were several holes in the plaster of the walls, bare boards showing through, and only one door. The room smelled of dust and damp.

"Oh, don't strain yourself. We're quite alone — for the moment. My colleagues are just outside. They'll come if called, so don't do anything foolish." Ervan sat back, crossed his legs, and tapped idly on his boot, fingers drumming.

"How could I do anything, foolish or otherwise? Your men have trussed me up like a pig on its way to the spit." Slowly, oh so slowly, Belasko started to work the rope that bound his wrists over the sharp point of the hook on the back of his chair. Belasko sighed. "Why are you doing this, Ervan? We both know I didn't have anything to do with Prince Kellan's death. Does your hatred of me burn so hot that you'd let the real killer go free to settle a personal vendetta?"

Ervan laughed. "You're priceless, Belasko. I have you exactly where I want you. Your escape from the palace cells only further incriminates you. And of course I want Kellan's killer to go free. It would hardly do to have one of his majesty's inquisitors in the cells now, would it?"

Belasko stared at the inquisitor. "What? *You* murdered the prince?"

Ervan relaxed further into his chair, leaning back and lacing his fingers together behind his head. "Well, I planned it. I found a most accommodating apothecary down here by the docks, implicated in a poisoning last year. They were only too happy to buy their freedom with a few helpful potions from time to time. A little help from someone in the kitchens eager to play a prank on the new girl certainly didn't go amiss. Unfortunately it seems that poor kitchen boy caught something dreadful while he was helping us with our inquiries, some illness or other he picked up in the cells, and he's not long for this world. What a dreadful shame that is."

Belasko couldn't believe what he was hearing. All the while Ervan talked, he worked to free his hands, could now feel strands of the rope fraying. He shook his head in shock. "I don't understand. I know from old that you're loyal to the crown, painfully so. I don't think you could have changed that much. How could you have planned the murder of the prince?"

The inquisitor sat forward suddenly, slamming his hands on the table with enough force that the rapier laid across it jumped. "It's precisely *because* I'm loyal, you idiot!" he shouted. "Kellan wasn't fit to rule. He was a drunk and a wastrel. He'd have pissed away the treasury on wine and whores, and bankrupted this country. No, Lilliana is the better choice."

"And who are you to make that decision?" Belasko asked quietly.

"Me? I might be the only sane man in a world of idiots. The one with the vision to see what must be done and carry it out, no matter the cost."

"I'm not sure Lilliana would agree with you. So what now? What will you do with me?"

Ervan grinned. "Oh you, my friend, are the icing on the cake. Not only was I able to ensure a suitable successor for King Mallor, I've been able to take you down at the same time. A life's ambition, achieved."

"I understand that you blame me for the loss of your eye. I didn't realise that your hatred ran so deep."

"You have no idea. It's not just you, it's what you represent." Ervan sneered at him. "Who are you to have the ear of kings? Some farmer's boy? No, it's past time that you were reminded of your place. You think you've been honoured because of your good looks and charm? You're exceptionally skilled with a blade, it's true, but that is all you are. A curiosity. A commoner that can beat a nobleman with a blade is like a talking dog, or some character from a travelling freak show."

Belasko could feel a few more of the strands of the rope that held him fray and part. He nodded at the rapier on the table. "What's that about, then?"

Ervan smiled. "I'm going to be the man that beats Belasko. My brave Inquisitors and I have tracked you down to this hideout in the docks, where we surprised you in the act of getting dressed up in your little disguise. When I attempted to arrest you, you resisted. You drew your blade against me and, after a fierce fight, I won out, running you through with my own trusty sword." His fingers caressed the hilt of the weapon he wore at his side.

"Won't people wonder where I got the sword, as mine was confiscated at the palace?" Belasko asked.

Ervan shrugged. "I'm sure you had it stashed here. You probably have weapons cached in hideouts all over the city, in the event that your plot to poison the prince went awry. People will believe that, I'm sure."

"So you're going to fight me?"

"Oh no," Ervan laughed, "I'm just going to run you through a few times while you're tied to that chair. Then, when you're dead, I'll put the rapier in your hand. I might have to give myself a few small wounds to make it believable, but I'll make sure you're dead first."

He stood and drew his sword. As Ervan came slowly around the table, relishing the moment, Belasko felt another strand of the rope give way. Dropping all pretence he pulled the rope against the sharp point of the hook with all his strength. Ervan laughed again. "Look at the great Belasko, frantic and fearful, desperate to escape. You should realise by now, there's no escape for you, there's — oh!"

The inquisitor could only let out an exclamation of surprise as Belasko heaved and the rope that held him snapped. He used his momentum to dive forwards over the table, away from Ervan, grabbing the rapier as he went. Belasko drew it from its scabbard as he landed in a ready position, ignoring as best he could a twinge of pain from his bad foot and gasping at a stab from his broken ribs. He still couldn't help but grin at the stricken look on the inquisitor's face. "Fancy trying to run me through now? You might find it more difficult in a fair fight."

Ervan kicked the table towards him and called for his men. An answering shout came from the next room, and the door crashed open. Two heavy-set men in black came through from the room beyond, one dark, one fair, each holding a pair of long knives, the sort that would be good for close work. They positioned themselves between Ervan and Belasko, and edged warily towards the duellist. Although they moved carefully there was no fear in their eyes. Belasko parried a thrust from one and then the other, as they sought to test his defences. As the fight began he saw Ervan run from the room.

"Damn it, Ervan! Come back and face me!" he roared, blade flickering fast as thought as he met his attackers' blows easily. He frowned and went on the attack. The men were skilled with their knives, and confident as they outnumbered him, but there was a reason Belasko had been the king's champion for so long. Blades glittered and shone in the dim light as Belasko tried to find a way through his opponents' defences, just as they tried to pierce his.

The men tried to split and step to either side of him, dividing his attention, but Belasko moved back into the room, keeping them both in front of him. He felt something at his back. *The table. I wonder...*

He lunged at them, blade flicking towards one set of eyes and then another. Just as quickly, he pushed himself back, onto the table, and did a backwards roll over it. His opponents went to rush around to either side, but as Belasko regained his feet he set himself against the table and sent it crashing into the darker of the knifemen, who went tumbling backwards. Belasko turned towards the fairer of the two, who was closing in on him fast. Setting his foot against the table, which now pinned the other knifeman to the wall, he pushed with all his might, causing a grunt of pain from the man against the wall, and propelling Belasko forward at great speed — a greater speed than his opponent was prepared for, his knives were too late to meet Belasko's challenge. Belasko reached out with his sword as he rose up and over the pair of knives and, almost negligently, slit the knifeman's throat. The weapons he had been holding fell to the ground, forgotten as frantic hands clutched at the gurgling, bloody mess that had been his neck.

The other man roared in anger, pushing the table away from himself. Belasko turned to face him. The knifeman went to vault the table and, as he sailed over it, Belasko went the other way and dropped down low, blade coming up to take his opponent in the groin, opening up the artery at the top of the thigh in the process. Another set of knives forgotten, the man in black whimpered as he tried to stem the spurting flow of blood that indicated a lethal wound had been made. Belasko knew from long experience that both men would bleed to death in moments.

He dashed from the room, through the adjoining chamber, and down some steps onto a wooden pavement. He scanned his surroundings but could see no trace of Inquisitor Ervan. It was only as he started to shiver that he realised he was still clad only in his smallclothes. Muttering to himself, he backed again into the hovel — which he could now see was a small house on a little-trafficked, narrow lane down by the docks — and quietly closed the door. He turned and surveyed the room for anything useful.

Fortunately they had brought along his clothes and the meagre possessions he had with him when captured, as well as the robe and walking stick that made up his disguise. He picked up the sheath and sword-belt that went with the rapier Ervan had planned to place on his corpse. Belasko quickly pulled on his clothes and buckled on the sword belt, taking a moment to appreciate the familiar weight at his side. Then he pulled the robe on over the top. He tied it loosely, so he could access the sword beneath, should he need it. Slinging the cloth bag Hibberth had given him over one shoulder, he picked up the walking stick and set out.

No sooner had he stepped outside then he heard the grating sound of wood scraping against wood, and a little voice hissed at him. "Oi, mister? You looking for an escape route by any chance?"

Belasko looked around him, puzzled at where the voice had come from.

"Down here mister, quick like."

Belasko looked down and, at the bottom of the steps to the little house, a section of the wooden walkway that made up the pavements had been lifted free. Appearing out of this hole, elbows propped on the edge, was what could only be described as an urchin. A filthy, scrawny child of indeterminate age and gender, who grinned up at Belasko in what would definitely be classed as a cheeky manner. Their hair may have been dark, it was difficult to tell under all the grime.

"That's right, down here. Need a hand getting away? Your friend Mr Inquisitor has already set the constables on you. Listen."

Belasko tilted his head, trying to make out anything over the background hubbub and clatter of the docks. Over the keening of the gulls he could just make out the thin piping of the whistles carried by the city watch — a sound that was growing louder and definitely closer.

Belasko frowned at the child. "I'm not exactly in a position to turn down help, but who are you?"

"Me?" The child's eyebrows arched, a humorous look on their face. "Oh, I'm nobody. Just a way out of a tight spot for you. But my boss wants a word. Reckons you can help each other out a bit."

"Boss? Who's that? What do they want?"

The child frowned. "Reckon you're better off asking them. I'm just supposed to offer you an escape route. Come with me and you'll get to ask them all the questions you like. Or you can stay here." They shrugged. "Up to you."

The whistles were louder, probably only a few streets away.

Belasko sighed. "Alright. I'm not even sure this is the oddest thing that's happened to me today. Mind out, I'm coming in." Belasko stepped up to the hole. Looking down, he could see a ladder that made its way down into the gloom. The urchin swung over to one side.

"You first," they said, "I've got to close up after."

Belasko swung his legs over the edge of the hole, feeling his way with his feet. Once they were securely on the ladder he turned, dropping down a couple of rungs until he had his hands on the ladder as well, and started to climb down.

"That's it. Don't go too far. Let me close this up and give your eyes a few moments to adjust."

Belasko stopped just below the child. He heard that same grating sound and the light from above dimmed and then was cut off. The child muttered and there was the sound of bolts being thrown.

"There you go. Now let your eyes adjust. We don't have to go too far down, but you'll want to be able to see as best you can once we're on the move."

Belasko did as he was bid and gradually he was able to make out a bit more of his surroundings, illuminated by the light that fell from gaps and cracks in the boardwalk above. He was perched on a ladder that dropped below him perhaps twice the height of a man, to a narrow ledge in what seemed to be some sort of borehole carved into the rock. Either side of the ledge two tunnels opened up, going in separate directions.

"Down you go, quick as quick can, but quiet like. We don't wanna alert the constables."

Belasko could hear the tread of heavy boots rattling the boardwalk above them. He nodded, and slid down the ladder as quietly as he could. When he got to the bottom he stood to one side, waiting for the child to climb down.

"Which way?" he whispered.

"Hang on a minute, let me shed a bit more light on the subject. Not too much mind, don't want to lose your vision." The child fished around underneath the ladder. "Here we go!" They brought out a shuttered lantern and opened one of the shutters a little, to illuminate the path in front of them. They grinned at Belasko and pointed the lantern down one of the tunnels.

"This way. Follow close behind." The child set off, not waiting to see if Belasko followed. "You should feel honoured, really," they called back over their shoulder. "There's not many as get summoned to meet his aquatic majesty."

9

Belasko almost stumbled as he set off to follow the child, surprised at what he'd just heard. "His aquatic... Hang on, are you saying you're taking me to meet the Water King?"

He could make out the child's shoulders giving a perfunctory shrug. "Reckon I might be. At least, that's what your lot call him."

"My lot? What do your lot call him then?"

The child laughed. "Nothing to his face. Not if we want to go to bed with the same amount of teeth we woke up with, that's for sure."

They were moving through a low tunnel, dug out of the earth and rock on which the city's docks had originally been built. Belasko had to duck from time to time, avoiding the low ceiling and its supporting beams. The only light now came from the lantern the child carried. The sound of water could be heard, trickling in the distance. Occasionally the openings of side passages appeared out of the gloom. His guide ignored these, keeping to the main tunnel.

"It's just," Belasko tripped slightly on the uneven floor, "I didn't think he existed. I — that is, everyone — thinks he's just a story."

"Reckon he likes it that way. You can ask him if he's real, if you like. He'd get a laugh out of that." The child paused at the entrance to one of the side passages, peering inside. They nodded and turned back to Belasko. "This way now. Stay close. It gets a bit twisty-turny from here. Wouldn't want to get separated. You'd be wandering around down here forever otherwise."

Belasko followed after them, going as quickly as he could, as his guide led him on a merry chase through a bewildering network of tunnels. There were turnings into other tunnels that came thick and fast. After a few minutes Belasko was completely disoriented and had no choice but to stick with the child. *There's no chance I could find my way back now.*

As well as losing his sense of distance, Belasko lost all sense of time as he hurtled along behind the child, turning this way and that under the earth. Eventually, it could have been hours later or only minutes, they spilled out into a large, dimly lit chamber. The child stopped in front of him and Belasko looked around, taking in his surroundings.

The chamber seemed large, the ceiling disappearing into shadow above them. The space was lit by more shuttered lanterns of the type the child carried, casting a dim glow. Belasko could make out other passageways that opened into the space and, at the far end, there was some sort of dais. On that dais was a shape that he couldn't quite make out. Belasko was aware of shadows moving around the edges of the room and realised that they weren't alone.

His guide moved into the cavernous space, beckoning Belasko to follow.

"Alright, our king? I fetched the fella you were after."

As they drew closer to the dais, a shadow lengthened and revealed itself to be a man, standing up from a chair that, to

Belasko, looked carved out of the rock itself. Gold teeth gleamed in a grin that cut through the gloom.

"Hello, Belasko. Welcome to the court of the Water King."

"Go on," hissed the child. "Approach." As Belasko walked forward they called out around him. "Alright, your aquatic majesty? Can I go now?"

That grin flashed again, followed by a booming laugh. "Begone child, attend to your work. Thank you for fetching my guest."

"Cheers." They turned to leave, pausing to wink at Belasko. "Reckon you'll do alright, mate. Just try not to piss him off." With that, the child was gone, disappearing back into the network of tunnels.

"Come closer Belasko, I don't bite. Well, not often. Come forward man, you're my guest! I've had food and drink brought for you. Come forward!"

As Belasko drew closer he could make out more of the figure. A barrel-chested man of middle years, his fingers and ears glistened with gold and silver rings. Long, curly black hair flowed down his back and his clothing was a riot of colour and clashing patterns. He wore a serviceable blade at his side. A glance was enough to tell Belasko that it was well-made and well-tended.

While the chair he had risen from was indeed carved from rock, it was supplemented with plenty of cushions and gaudy throws. In front of him was a table laden with food, and another chair, to which the man gestured.

"Sit, sit, take your ease. Trust me, your seat is more comfortable than this bloody thing." The man waved at the mass of rock behind him. "I know, I know, you'd hardly expect a man of my reputation to pad things out with a few cushions. But honestly, at my age this bloody thing is just an invitation to piles. Nobody wants that."

Belasko took the chair he had been offered, eyeing the man

before him warily. The strange man picked up a goblet from the table and settled back onto his cushions, nonchalantly cocking one dangling leg over the arm of the stony throne.

"You're the Water King?"

The man laughed again, the sound echoing around the chamber. "Not as quick on the uptake as I thought you'd be. Still that's to be expected after the last few days. Now come on, help yourself to whatever you want. We don't stand on ceremony here."

Belasko sat still for a moment, not sure what to say next. "It's just... well, I didn't think you really existed. Nobody does. I thought you were just some fairy tale. Something to tell children to scare them into good behaviour."

A knowing smile now, not the broad grin. The Water King leaned forward conspiratorially, raising an eyebrow. "Don't you think that's just the way I like it? You high muckety mucks up at the palace think I'm some sort of myth. Means you leave me alone so I can get on with my work in peace."

Belasko leaned forward, picking up a goblet of his own. He sniffed it first, then carefully replaced it on the table. "I'm sorry, and please don't think me rude, but the last wine I was offered was drugged. That was given to me by an old friend, and we've only just met. So I hope you'll forgive me for being a little wary."

"Not at all, very sensible. Here." The Water King leaned forward and, picking up Belasko's goblet, took a healthy swallow. "There, perfectly safe. I'll drink what you drink, eat what you eat. I wouldn't very well poison myself now, would I? Out of curiosity, what is it you lot up there currently believe about me?" He passed the goblet back to Belasko.

Belasko shrugged, taking a sip of wine. "No one knows anything for certain. Some people say you're the disgraced son of a foreign nobleman. Others a former pirate that gave up the sea. Some say you're ten feet tall and half-man, half-sea monster. A beast of magic and misadventure. All sorts, really. The only thing they can agree on is that you rule the criminal element of the city with an iron fist."

The Water King smiled slyly. "Oh, I don't know about an iron fist. I dole out my share of tough love to my subordinates, sometimes tougher than others. As for magic... Well, I used to have a Vargossian shaman in my employ. He could be quite effective, on the rare occasion you'd find him either sober, conscious, or both. One of your stories is close to the truth, though."

"Which one?"

"Well, I wouldn't want to go into all the gory details, but I was once a pirate. A smuggler, really. A smuggler that came to stay. I soon realised that if I controlled the docks, I could control the flow of contraband in and out of the city, so I set about taking it over from the existing crime lords of the day. Over time I expanded my sphere of control and now there isn't a crime in the city I don't know about — or at least a share of the booty ends up in my pocket."

The Water King leaned forward, piling foodstuffs onto a plate.

"But you see, the current situation is very bad for business. It's very sad, what happened to the prince, but I can't abide all these searches at the city gates. It's making it hard for a dishonest man to make a living. Dishonest women too, for that matter."

He sat back, balancing the plate on one leg as he started to pick at his food. "So tell me: did you murder the prince?"

Belasko shook his head. "No."

"I thought not. Belasko, I have a proposal for you. If I help you, and you discover the real murderer, all of our lives can go back to normal. The conditions are, you forget anything you learn about me and my operation in the process. Also, you owe me a favour, just one, that I may or may not claim at some point in the future. How does that sound?"

Belasko leaned forward and, only taking from foods the Water King had already selected, started piling food onto his own plate. Watching the other man eat had made him aware that he was incredibly hungry.

"That sounds alright," he said around a mouthful of cheese and bread. He winced in pain as the food found the still raw gap of his missing tooth, and swallowed. "As long as you know that I'll never do anything to harm the royal family or this country. If your future favour requires anything like that of me, then I won't do it. Agreed?" The Water King nodded. "Good. The thing is, I've already discovered who the real killer is — well, who ordered the murder anyway. What I need now is help tracking down the person who can prove it: the apothecary that gave them the poison."

Belasko concentrated on his food for a moment, only looking up from his plate when he realised his host had gone silent. The Water King looked shocked. He leaned forward. "You already know who did it? How did you find out? Tell me everything you know."

Around further mouthfuls of food, Belasko filled him in on the events of the day and Ervan's confession. The Water King was silent throughout.

"And that's when your, um, colleague found me and brought me down here. What do you think? Can you help me find the apothecary's shop?"

The Water King waved away the enquiry. "Oh, that's easy. I already know the one the inquisitor was talking about. It's just... You know what angers me? Amateurs. Bloody amateurs!" His voice echoed around the chamber. "What was the point of him telling you everything before he killed you? There's no need. I mean, it's handy for us because now we know where to go, but who does that? You don't grandstand and show off how clever you've been when you've got somebody to kill. Just kill them! Then you can pat yourself on the back for your brilliance afterwards. If you want to boast, do it afterwards to your henchmen, that's what they're for. Bloody amateurs. Just be glad it wasn't me that wanted you dead, you'd already be five fathoms deep, throat slit, stones tied to your feet." He shook his head. "Bloody amateurs."

Belasko stared at him. "While I've proven quite hard to kill over the years, do remind me not to get on your bad side."

That grin flashed again. "Oh, don't you worry. Our interests are aligned. You want this whole mess over and the status quo returned, as do I. And while I'm in a bad business, I'm not a bad sort. Not really." Now the Water King was serious. "From what the inquisitor said, you're looking for an apothecary called Azra. A bitter old bastard, I've found his services useful myself a time or two, though I had no idea it was an inquisitor that cleared up that little mess for him a while back. I was annoyed about it at the time — he'd taken it on as unsanctioned work you see. I'll see if Nobody is still about, they'll be able to guide you there quickest. Oi!" He leaned back in his seat, gesturing to someone unseen in the shadows. A gaunt-looking woman in drab grey clothes came forward, eyes hard and sharp as flint. "Fetch that little pipsqueak, will you? I need them to take our friend here somewhere up top." The woman nodded, silent, and glided away.

Belasko frowned. "'Nobody'? Are you telling me their name is Nobody? I thought they were making a joke."

"They were in a way. See, when they came to me a few years ago, them and their twin, even scrawnier than they are now, I asked them their names. 'Nobody and No One,' they said. Orphans, mostly brought themselves up on the street. Either they don't know the names their mother gave them or they don't care. Either way, it started as a joke but seems to have stuck. Ah, here they are now. Like two sides of the same grubby coin."

Belasko's earlier guide came slinking out of the shadows accompanied by another child. No One was slightly taller, and fair where Nobody was dark, but with an unmistakably similar cast to their features. "Hello Nobody," he greeted them, "and No One, I presume?"

No One nodded in response. Nobody winked at Belasko and gave him a cheeky grin. "Alright, mate? Getting along okay with the big boss, are you?"

The Water King leaned forward on his stony throne. "That he is. Now make yourself useful before I decide to sell you to some drunken sailor as a pair of pet monkeys. Our friend here needs to get to Azra's apothecary shop. You know the one? A couple of streets over from that cheap jewellers you burgled last year, just back from the docks." Both of the children nodded. "Good. Get him there, help him grab the apothecary, and bring them back here. Understand?"

The children both gave a deep bow, solemnly intoning, "Yes, our aquatic majesty. Your wish is our command," as they did so.

"Cheeky buggers," the Water King muttered under his breath, although the look he gave the children seemed full of genuine affection. He looked back to Belasko. "Ready?"

It was as confusing a journey back to the surface as it had been entering the Water King's underworld in the first place. Full of twists and turns, the children led the way unerringly, cutting through the darkness like a blade's edge catching moonlight.

Before long they arrived at a ladder that climbed up to the city above. The children shinned up it first, knocking on the boards at the top in a prearranged pattern. After a moment there came a series of knocks in reply. Nobody, who had led the way, undid the bolts that secured the underside of the hatch and then someone above slid it free. Light poured into the tunnel and a curious face peered down. It recognised the children and smiled.

"Hello, you two. I see you've brought a guest. Well, up you come."

A meaty hand reached down and pulled up Nobody, then No One. Belasko climbed the ladder and took the same hand when it was offered to him. He was surprised to find himself lifted bodily out of the tunnel, whoever was helping them taking almost all of his weight without complaint. He was lifted out into a small, dusty storeroom with a few desultory barrels and crates stacked up around its edges, and he saw his helper. Broad. That was the only way to describe him. And tall. Very tall. Thick of waist but broader of shoulder, with shaggy, dun-coloured hair and an air of amiability that probably came easily when your strength was rarely challenged.

He smiled at Belasko and shook the hand he still held. "Hello. Borne's the name. Any friend of these two reprobates is a friend of mine."

"Nice to meet you." Belasko looked around him. "Where are we?"

"The tunnels are confusing, aren't they? You're in a warehouse by the docks, owned by someone I'm guessing is a mutual acquaintance, or you wouldn't have used this entrance. Now, you'd better be off on whatever business you're about."

The big man bent down to push the hatch cover back into place. Then he moved over to a simple wooden chair in the corner of the room. Picking up a fat book that sat atop a nearby crate, he took a seat. He thumbed through it, trying to find his place.

"How's the book?" asked No One.

Borne lifted up the volume he was holding. "This one is most enjoyable, a compendium of Villanese verse from the last century." His face took on a more serious expression. "It wouldn't do you two any harm to pick up a book occasionally, undertake a little learning. Now, will you be coming back this way anytime soon?"

Nobody pointed at Belasko. "Depends on him. Shouldn't be long. Just got to grab someone and head back down."

Borne nodded, head already dipping as he turned back to his book. "Good, good. Off you go, then."

They slipped out of the storeroom and into the warehouse beyond, Borne already oblivious to their presence.

Belasko waited across the road from the apothecary's shop, leaning against a wall as casual as could be. It seemed like it was empty, or at least closed for the day. There were no customers going in or out, although a number of people passed by on foot and the road was busy with carts and carriages.

I'd best get word to Orren somehow. Let him know I'm on to something. Where to find me. He looked down at the children. "Would you two like to earn some extra coin while I wait? By taking a message for me?"

The children looked at each other before eyeing him suspiciously. "Our watery boss said to bring you up here, then to bring you back with the apothecary — not go running off and leaving you on your own," said No One.

Belasko shook his head. "I just need you to take a message and, hopefully, return with a friend of mine. A bit of extra muscle in case the apothecary doesn't want to come willingly. If it makes you feel any better, I promise I won't go in until you return."

The children looked at each other again, some silent agreement passing between them.

"How much coin?" asked Nobody.

"Yeah, how much?" asked No One.

"Oh, I should say at least five pennies each. Does that sound good?"

"Too good," said No One. "What's the catch?"

Belasko shook his head. "No catch, I'm just in a hurry to get on with our business and am willing to pay for speed of delivery. You two can run fast, can't you?"

"Faster than the wind, that's us." Nobody grinned. "What's the message and where to?"

"Go to the Weeping Anchor Inn, do you know it?" They both nodded. "Good. Find a man there called Orren — he's a big man, with a big mess of blonde hair. Tell him that his old friend has found what he's been looking for, then bring him back here as quickly as you can. Does that sound alright?" The children nodded again. Belasko fumbled in his bag and withdrew some shining coins. "Here you go. Five pennies now, and my friend will pay you the rest once you've brought him back here. Now off you go, quick as you can."

The twins sped off down the street and Belasko eyed the door to the apothecary's shop, a feeling of hope rising in his chest.

I'm getting somewhere at last.

10

Time dragged as Belasko waited. His anxiety increased with every moment that passed, fear that the apothecary wouldn't be there, or had already got away. Proof of Ervan's guilt and his own innocence was within his grasp, and he was desperate not to let it slip through his fingers. He began to imagine Orren being suspicious of his chosen messengers, turning them away. Or worse, that he had for some reason had to leave the Weeping Anchor and couldn't be found.

Belasko shook his head, as if to knock these thoughts out of it. *He'll be there. Come on Orren, trust the children. Come here quick as you can.*

As he waited he thought back to the early days of his and Orren's friendship, as two new recruits paired up in training. As they had talked they found out that they were both farmers' sons, both ran away to join the army.

One night, around a campfire, conversation had turned to why they joined up. Belasko had poked the fire with a stick, then leant back on his elbows. He smiled into the firelight, its reflection gleaming in his eyes. "It was glory that did it for me. The bright uniform of the recruiting sergeant, his talk of serving king and country." He snorted. "That and fear. Fear of living a life as dull as my parents'. Breaking my back with constant toil just to see all my hard work undone by drought or bad luck. Fear of being different, that I wouldn't be accepted for who I am. There weren't exactly many like me in our village, if you take my meaning. How about you?"

Orren was sat further back, face in shadow. "Well, my da's a bit of a bastard. Nasty man. Beat me and my brothers and sisters every day, for some imagined insult, or disrespecting him by not attending to our chores properly. So I ran away. One day soon, when I'm on leave, I'm going to go back there in my uniform, with my sword, and put the fear of God into him so he never touches any of them again. Once I'm earning a good wage as a soldier I can get them away from him, set them up somewhere else. Do right by them. If I'd stayed I'd likely have killed him and been hung for it. I'm no good to any of them dead."

Belasko had swallowed. "We've all got our reasons."

As Belasko loitered, the building feeling of impatience brought him back to the present day and almost got the better of him. He was about to push off from the wall across from the shop and make his way over the street. As casually as possible, he reached inside his robe and adjusted his rapier in its scabbard, making it easier to draw if needed.

Then in the distance he made out a familiar figure, shaggy blonde hair standing out above the crowd. Belasko couldn't help grinning to himself. His big friend was being towed through the crowd by the two children, who led him straight to Belasko's side.

Orren grinned at him. "Hello, friend. My, you've fallen from the priestly station I last saw you occupying."

"You don't know the half of it," Belasko said as the two men clasped hands. "And I'll tell you all about it after we're done here. What kept you, by the way?" He looked at Nobody and No One. "You said you'd be quick. It felt like I waited an age."

"It's not their fault," Orren interjected. "The doorman wouldn't let them in at first. It was only when they mentioned me by name and described me that he relented. They brought me as quick as they could, said you'd promised them I'd pay ten pennies for the privilege."

Belasko raised an eyebrow. "They did, did they?" Nobody and No One looked up at him, faces a picture of innocence.

"Well," said Nobody, "I couldn't remember if you said ten pennies from him, or ten pennies total. Rubbish with figures, I am."

"Me too," said No One. "Numbers aren't our strong suit. On account of our lack of schooling."

Belasko sighed, shaking his head in rueful amusement. "Well, I'm sure you earned it."

"Sorry to interrupt, but what are we about? I'm glad to see you, but what are we doing?"

"I've got a lot to tell you," said Belasko, "but for now all you need to know is that in that shop is the apothecary that supplied the poison that was used to kill Prince Kellan. They can help us prove who the real killer is."

"So what are we waiting for? Let's go and get them."

"Yes, let's. You two." Belasko pointed at Nobody and No One. "Wait here, across the road. We'll go in and grab the apothecary, then you can whisk us away and back to your boss. If anyone else comes out of there before we do, one of you follow them. Discretely. The other, run back to your boss as quick as you can and come back with reinforcements. We'll likely be in trouble. Understood?" They both nodded. "Good. Right, shall we go in?"

Although the shop looked closed from the outside, the door swung open easily, setting off a chime from a small bell that was fixed to the top of the door. Belasko and Orren paused for a moment but, hearing nothing stirring inside the shop, carried on and walked inside.

It took a few moments for his eyes to adjust from the bright daylight outside, but when they did Belasko was shocked by the sight before him. The apothecary's shop had been ransacked. Tables and cabinets over-turned, jars smashed, herbs and valuable tinctures spilled across the floor. The smell of all the spilled potions and ingredients was quite staggering.

Belasko turned to Orren, gesturing for them both to remain silent, and they moved further into the shop. They tried not to disturb the detritus spread across the floor, ears straining to catch the sound of any movement, breath loud in their own ears.

"Azra?" Belasko called as he moved through the shop. "Are you here? We came to see if you could help us with something. Are you well?"

Against the wall to Belasko's right was a counter, behind which was a door into another room — from which they heard a scratching sound. Before Belasko could even think about it, he had vaulted the counter, wincing as he landed on his bad foot, stumbling slightly as the transfer of weight sent a white hot blast of pain through his broken ribs, and drew his rapier. He pushed open the door and slipped through, calling out, "Azra, are you there?" as he went.

It was darker still in the back room, but his eyes were quick to adjust. A yowling streak of fur bolted past him and through the door as a cat made its bid for freedom. Then he noticed the dark puddle on the floor against the back wall, the red that had splashed up the wall, the crumpled figure lying amidst it all.

Orren followed Belasko into the room and swore under his breath. Belasko made his way over to the body and crouched to inspect it, putting his rapier down to one side as he did so. It was a man, though he had been butchered so badly that it was difficult to see the person he was in life.

"What's the betting that's our apothecary?" Orren asked.

Belasko shook his head. "It can only be him, I'm sure of it."

The bell above the shop door rang out again. Belasko and Orren exchanged looks.

"Were you expecting company?" asked Orren.

"No, and I'm sure the two children wouldn't come in without calling out fair warning," said Belasko, picking up his rapier as he stood up. Orren also drew his sword and the two men readied themselves, prepared to fight by each other's side in a way that was almost instinctive after all the years they had spent together.

Belasko heard at least two sets of footsteps and frowned. *Too heavy to be the children.* The door opened and three members of the city watch walked in. They took in the mess of the room, the dead body with Belasko and Orren standing over it, all with wide eyes.

One of them whistled. "You really messed this place up, didn't you? Made a mess of them and all." He nodded towards the apothecary's corpse as he and his two colleagues drew the short swords that hung at their belts.

"No, we didn't! We only just got here, the same as you. Look." Belasko held up his rapier. "I don't have blood on my blade, neither does he. Whatever was used on him, it was heavier than my sword."

The three men edged towards him, spreading out as they did so.

"That's all well and good," the watchman said, "but I'm sure we'd all feel better if you put those down and came with us. Someone tipped us off that this shop had been turned over and that we'd best come quick. I'm glad we listened."

One of the others was frowning intently, staring at Belasko. A light of recognition dawned in their eyes. "Sarge," they hissed, "it's him. The one we've been looking for. The duellist."

Their leader swallowed. "I think you're right. Listen, we've orders to arrest you on sight. We'll sort out what's happened here afterwards. You're wanted for poisoning Prince Kellan. Now give up your swords and come with us."

"No," said Belasko, standing firm. "We won't be going with you or putting down our swords. You're going to let us go. We'd hate to have to hurt you."

The watchman laughed nervously, forcing a grin for his colleagues' benefit. "Oh, I'm sure you would. In case you hadn't noticed, though, we outnumber you."

Orren shrugged. "We've faced worse odds."

As he spoke, Belasko sprang forward, lunging at the watchman to his right, blade flicking out to probe his defences, and then redirected the blow towards the man in the centre. Their opponents parried and riposted, and battle was joined.

It is odd, Belasko thought to himself, *to be fighting whilst trying so hard not to hurt your opponents. Particularly when they share no such compunction towards you.*

Belasko's blade wove a dazzling network of steel, keeping two of their three opponents at bay, but it was difficult to manoeuvre in such tight quarters. The short swords the watchmen carried were better suited to the close conditions of their fight, but the greater reach of Belasko and Orren's blades kept them from pressing their advantage. There also wasn't really anywhere for he and Orren to go — for every inch of ground they gained on their strange battlefield they lost another. They were struggling to create an avenue of escape. The combatants edged forwards and back, blades ringing out as they danced their futile steps, the movements of the watchmen clumsy in comparison to Orren and Belasko's.

"Try not to hurt them," he shouted to Orren over the clashing steel as his friend blocked a blow from his opponent almost nonchalantly. "They're only doing their duty."

"They don't seem to have any such compunction, my friend. Shall we leave? Let's go around rather than through."

With a great deal of effort, by working together in a partnership that had been decades in the making, Belasko and Orren managed to gradually turn the fight around. One crept closer to the other, who would then inch across to one side, so that little by little they moved around the room and were eventually edging towards the door. They knew each others' fighting style inside out and could communicate with a look or glance. Belasko caught his friend's eye and nodded. They would need to move quickly, get out the door and try to trap the watchmen inside, or else fight them to a standstill.

As one, Belasko and Orren broke off the fight and went to dash through the door. When Belasko put his weight on his bad foot, his body, exhausted after the efforts of the last few days, betrayed him. Pain shot through him and he stumbled. It wasn't much but it allowed one of the watchmen an opening — an opening that they took, launching a desperate thrust of their short sword.

Belasko never felt the touch of his enemy's blade, because Orren, without thinking, put himself between his friend and harm's way. He dived in front of the watchman's thrust and took the blow meant for Belasko. The short sword pierced his side below the ribs, thrust deep, and both Orren and Belasko knew it was a killing wound. A look of shock crossed Orren's face, and he twisted to face Belasko as he fell to the ground. "Run, you fool!" he managed to gasp, blood flowing from his injury. "Just bloody run!"

And run Belasko did. Away from the shouts of the watchmen. Away from the sight of his best friend dying on the floor. Away from the chaos of the apothecary's shop. But he couldn't run from the pain, the deep sense of loss opening up inside him. He couldn't run from the guilt.

11

Lilliana ducked into her father's study. The hour was late, but she had managed to convince her personal guard that there was something she desperately needed for her studies. Unfortunately she'd been unable to find the tome she needed in the library — would they mind waiting for a moment while she checked to see if it was in her father's study? The patient, and no doubt tired and eager to be relieved, guards were standing fast outside the door.

Where is it?

Her father and Inquisitor Ervan were making much of this letter that had been found in her father's apartments, the one which supposedly incriminated Belasko. Lilliana knew it must be a nonsense, but had to see for herself.

Otherwise, what have I done in freeing Belasko? What if he is *the murderer and I'm the one he's managed to fool.*

She lifted the small lantern she carried, illuminating her father's desk. It was normally very neatly arranged, everything in its proper place. It was almost unrecognisable now. Papers strewn across its surface, everything in disorder.

Oh Father, this is so unlike you. Lilliana's lips curled in a sad smile. *On the bright side it means I won't have to work hard to cover my tracks.*

She carefully placed her lantern where it would cast light over the desk, then bent over it and started to rifle through the papers scattered so casually. Frowning, unable to find what she was looking for, she started to go through the desk's drawers. She went through each as quickly as she could while still being thorough, but still couldn't find what she was looking for. Frustrated, she yanked open the bottom drawer. And there, sitting on top of a stack of other papers, was a letter. A letter with Belasko's seal on it.

Hands shaking, she removed the letter. It had already been opened and read, more than once by the look of the creases in it. She started to read, a frown on her face.

"*My dear King Mallor,*" it read, "*I must beg your forgiveness for an unforgivable act. My dearest concern has ever been the welfare of yourself and the Villanese nation and people. It tears at me to see so you so troubled by the actions of your son, and my friend, Prince Kellan. As dear as he is to you, and to me, it is clear that he is not fit to rule. Hot-headed, undisciplined, lazy, a drunkard who idles away his days in the company of other drunks and whores, he is not the heir you deserve.*

"*Rather, look to your daughter, Princess Lilliana. She has all the qualities Kellan lacks. Calm, intelligent, rational, a strong young woman who can weigh arguments and find solutions. She is the heir that you and the country need.*

"*So, this evening, I have done my final duty for the sake of the Villanese people and nation. I have murdered your son.*"

The letter rambled on in this vein at some length. As she reached its end, Lilliana's eyes welled up and tears began to run down her cheeks. After a few moments she cleared her throat, wiping her eyes with her sleeve. *Still, there's one consolation. This isn't Belasko's handwriting.*

She turned the letter over. The seal was genuine, the

crossed blades of the royal champion, as was the signature. But the contents? That was someone else's work.

Lilliana hesitated, then stuffed the letter into a pocket inside her cloak. She closed the drawer and scanned the desk to make sure she hadn't upset the disorder too much. *Quickly now, before you lose your nerve.*

She picked up the lantern and made her way over to the study door, opening it quietly. The two guards stationed to either side turned to her. One, smiling, asked, "Did you find what you were looking for, your highness?" Then he saw her expression and his face fell.

Lilliana smiled sadly at them. "I didn't find quite what I was looking for, but something that reminded me of my brother instead. I'm alright. Thank you. Would you escort me back to my rooms now, please? I feel very tired all of a sudden."

Ambassador Aveyard sat before the fireplace in the lounge attached to her private chambers. Although it was only autumn, she was still not accustomed to the colder climate of this northern country and so was swathed in robes as she sipped brandy and caught up on some personal reading before bed. There came a knock at the door. She sighed, closing her book and setting it down on a table beside her chair, although she didn't put down her brandy.

"Come," she called, knowing as she did so who would be at her door.

The door opened to reveal Jonteer, her secretary and spymaster. The firelight reflected in his cold, grey eyes as he gave her a perfunctory bow. His uniform was immaculate, even this late at night. *Does the man never sleep?*

"Madam Ambassador, my apologies for disturbing you at

this late hour. I've had a communication from the palace that I thought I had better share with you immediately."

"Oh?" Aveyard sipped her brandy. "Then you better had. What does the palace want?"

Jonteer cleared his throat. "You have been asked to attend the king tomorrow night for informal talks in his private audience chamber."

"Informal talks? On what subject?"

"That wasn't entirely clear." Jonteer frowned. "The letter I received expressed an interest in furthering a peaceful relationship between our two countries, coming to some sort of... permanent arrangement."

Aveyard's eyebrows shot up as she looked at Jonteer over the rim of her brandy glass, from which she now took a healthy swallow. "A permanent arrangement? What in heaven can that mean? Some sort of treaty?"

Jonteer edged further into the room, closing the door behind him. "One thing does occur to me, my lady."

Aveyard drained her brandy glass, setting the empty vessel down on top of her now abandoned book. "Go on."

"With Prince Kellan dead and Princess Lilliana as heir, the king may be feeling the need to secure the succession further. By marriage, and production of a grandchild."

Aveyard laughed. "You think that wily old King Mallor wants to marry off his only daughter, his only remaining child, to who? A member of the Baskan royal house? That his people fought a devastating war against in living memory?"

"Not marry off as such, no." Jonteer shook his head. "But an alliance between the two houses would help build a more peaceful relationship between our peoples. There is no way they would accept someone to rule over Princess Lilliana, but a lesser son as some sort of Prince Consort? It's entirely possible. Villan has secured their relationship with other neighbours by marriage in the past. As to the other point, after the Last War, some would have thought it unlikely that Baskans would be welcome in Villan at all, but the world moves on. Trade is as important as ever it was and it is often money that dictates political decision making. It's just something to bear in mind, when you attend the king tomorrow. If it comes up, you wouldn't want the subject to come as a complete surprise."

There was a moment of silence, Ambassador Aveyard looking into the fireplace. She sighed, then looked back up at her secretary. "I'd ask for your reassurance that we had nothing to do with Prince Kellan's death, that this wasn't part of some grand plan, but I know you wouldn't answer me honestly either way." Jonteer's eyes gleamed in the firelight as he regarded the ambassador, silent. Aveyard shook her head. "Whether it was planned or just an opportunity to be seized, I will bear your thoughts in mind tomorrow, at the palace. Thank you for bringing me word of the invitation, you're right that I would want to know immediately. Is there anything else?"

Jonteer frowned. "I have heard something, about a commotion near the docks this morning. It's not public yet, but it seems like Belasko had a confrontation with several members of the Inquisition."

"Really?" Aveyard leaned forward in her seat. "So Belasko is still in the city, he hasn't fled?"

Jonteer shook his head. "No. According to the Inquisition several of their number, led by Inquisitor Ervan, surprised Belasko at a hideout he was using. There was a fight and two of the Inquisition are dead. Ervan survived to search for reinforcements, but by the time he returned with some of the city watch Belasko had disappeared again."

"Is there no indication of where he may have gone?"

"None. In the words of one present, 'It was as if the ground opened up and swallowed him.'"

"Interesting." Aveyard rubbed her chin. "Why would he still

be in the city? Surely he should be halfway to the border by now. Unless ..."

"Yes, my lady?"

"Unless he has reason to stay behind. Unfinished business. Perhaps he is innocent, or is seeking revenge. Interesting. Thank you for bringing this to me. Do keep your eyes and ears open. Let me know as soon as you hear anything else. Belasko's actions intrigue me. Is there anything else I should know?" Jonteer shook his head. "Very well. Good night, Jonteer."

He saluted her, heels clicking together. "Good night, my lady." Then he turned and left, closing the door gently behind him.

Aveyard waited for a moment then, taking her glass, rose and went over to a crystal decanter that sat on a small side table. She poured herself another generous measure of brandy and went to stand in front of the fireplace, soaking up the heat it gave off.

Damn this cold place. How I long for the heat of my southern home again. And to be rid of all this scheming and politicking.

Belasko looked down at the pale face of his dead friend. *It should have been me.*

As was tradition, Orren's body had been taken to the nearest chapel of the dead. It didn't matter how he had died, whether killed in a fight with the city watch or passing peacefully in his sleep, the correct rites were observed. His body would lie in the chapel overnight. In the morning the watch would return and claim the body, try to identify him, but for now he lay undisturbed and Belasko was able to sit vigil over the body, as was also tradition. He had gone to the chapel alone, sending Nobody and No One back to their master.

It was an austere place, a simple room of cut stone with no

comfort in it. A bier stood in the centre of the room, on which Orren's body lay, covered by a shroud. Candles in wall sconces gave a flickering light, doing nothing to banish the shadows that pooled in the corners.

Neither watch nor chapel knew exactly who lay in state that night. It was quite common in such instances that pious members of the local community would sit vigil in the absence of a friend or loved one. It had been the work of moments for Belasko to convince a priest that he was such a kind-hearted individual.

"Here, a donation for the chapel." A glint of light as some coins changed hands. "It's the least I can do. I hope someone will do the same for me when the time comes."

The priest had nodded. "Quite right, my son. You do yourself a credit in the eyes of Aronos. Please, come in." Belasko had been ushered into the chapel. The priest left him, murmuring only that someone would be along at dawn to show him out.

Belasko reached out and stroked Orren's brow, smoothing out his shaggy blonde hair. *It's all my fault.*

"I'm so sorry, my friend. I'll look after Denna and the children, I promise. And the man responsible for all our woes, that bastard Ervan, I'll see him dead for this," Belasko whispered, repeating the thoughts that were running around and around in his mind. He sighed.

But is Ervan responsible? He killed the prince and set me up, but I didn't have to stay to try and clear my name.

"I should have listened to you; should have left when I had the chance. We both should have."

You had to be the hero didn't you? Run around the city trying to solve the murder, trying to regain your reputation, save what you have built. What does any of that matter now?

"Everything I have, I built with you. You should be the one in the stories and songs. We built it all together from the start."

Belasko sat for a long time as the night turned cold, and watched over his friend's body by the flickering candlelight.

Memories of Orren ran continuously through his mind. The many kindnesses he showed to others. His dry, mocking sense of humour. The loyalty he had shown to all his friends and loved ones.

And where did your loyalty get you?

"Dead, because of my arrogance."

Too late to run now. Your best friend is dead. You know who killed the prince. You just have to do something about it. Orren would have wanted you to see this through.

Belasko tipped his head back against the wall and closed his eyes.

"I'm going to get Ervan for this, for all of this. Not for me, for my pride, or to defend my position or what I've built. None of that matters. I'm going to do it for you, because your death deserves justice, and for Kendra, because she deserves better than being used as a pawn in Ervan's scheme."

He opened his eyes and stood, walking back to Orren's body and placing a hand palm-down on his chest.

"I don't care if I lose it all. Justice will be done."

The priest returned with the dawn, opening the chamber to find Belasko sitting cross-legged on the floor at the head of the bier on which Orren's body rested. His head was lowered, hood up, as he mumbled to himself.

"How are you, my child?"

Belasko stood slowly, feeling all of his aches and pains with every movement. "I'm well, Father. Thank you."

"And what were you saying to yourself just now, as I came in? I couldn't quite make it out."

A smile spread across Belasko's face, unseen under his hood. It was grim, with no humour in it. "A prayer, Father. A prayer for justice."

12

Belasko had resolved himself to his next course of action. He set off for Lord Hibberth's house, as it was on his way, walking stick click-clacking on the cobblestones. The journey took far longer than it would have normally, as Belasko had to avoid the notice of the watch. *For every step forward I have to take three to the side. Or climb up to the rooftops. Or lower myself into a sewer. There have to be better ways to travel.*

Dawn was well past and the day was marching on by the time he approached the back door to Hibberth's house. Having successfully avoided the city watch, he'd spent a little time observing the house, trying to make sure there would be no unpleasant surprises when he knocked on the door. Satisfied that the risk was minimal, he walked up and knocked on the back door.

After a few moments Meerling opened the door. He frowned at the apparent beggar on the doorstop. "Why do we seem to be attracting so many vagrants these days?" He sighed. "Alright, what can I do for you?"

"Your master, Lord Hibberth. I have a message for him."

"Well then," Meerling held out his hand, "pass it over and I'll see that he gets it."

Belasko shook his head. "It's not written down. I've got it up here." Belasko reached up and tapped the side of his head through the hood of his robe. "I'm to tell it to the lord, no one else."

Meerling looked affronted. "Well, this is happening a little too often lately for my liking. You wait here. I'll go and tell my master, and see what he wishes to do." The servant closed the door in his face.

A few moments passed, then the door opened and Hibberth's round face was revealed as he peered out into the darkening night, trying to see if there was anyone else nearby. He frowned. "You can't be here," he hissed. "I can't give you shelter."

"Why?"

"What, apart from the fact that you're on the run, accused of murdering our prince? Besides that, word of your antics down by the docks is already spreading through the city. You killed two of his majesty's Inquisition."

"They attacked me. I was defending myself!"

Hibberth sighed. "Do you think that's the story that's going around? Or do you think that a certain one-eyed inquisitor might just be telling people that you were resisting arrest? That only confirms your guilt in the eyes of many, even more so than escaping the cells." His eyes narrowed. "You didn't explain how you managed that, by the way."

Belasko snorted. "Nor will I. Look, I didn't come here for shelter but to let you know." He swallowed. "Orren is dead. Killed while helping me."

Hibberth paled, fear and shock mixing in his eyes. "What?"

"There will be more deaths before this is over," Belasko said quietly. "I intend to ensure that one of those killed is the true murderer of Prince Kellan. I have money, lodged at the banking houses, in Orren's name. If anything happens to me, see it reaches his wife and children. Now stay safe in your house, Hibberth. Wait for all this to blow over. I won't forget the help you already gave me. I'll remember the part you played in bringing the killer to justice."

"See that you do. Now get off my doorstep." Hibberth, visibly shaken, stepped back and swung the door shut with enough force to rattle the frame.

Belasko backed away, turned, and was gone.

Belasko looked up at the palace gates and swallowed, suddenly nervous.

What if they check people coming in for the ceremony? He shook his head. *If they do it's out of your control anyway.*

The palace guard worked in shifts of two weeks on, one week off, with three companies of guards rotating regularly to keep them fresh, and alert. That was the idea, anyway. Once a week a ceremony took place, the incoming guard meeting the outgoing guard so their commanders could exchange keys. What had no doubt started as a fairly simple handover of duties had, with the gentle accruing of time, become more of a show. The incoming and outgoing guard, uniforms immaculate, would march around each other in the parade ground inside the palace gates, while their commanders exchanged keys and ritual words in the centre of the square.

Of course there were other guards still on duty, but attention was on the square, not on the crowd which always gathered to watch. They were permitted into the parade square, but no further. Not into the palace proper.

It's all I need. It's a way in.

Belasko pushed himself further into the crowd that was heading through the gate. He walked with a limp that was not affected, his foot paining him greatly, his walking stick tapping along the ground. He pulled his hood down further.

When Nobody and No One had returned him to the Water King's lair after the disaster at the apothecary's shop, they had all sat in silence for a while after Belasko recounted what had happened.

The Water King's fingers drummed on the arm of his throne. "What now?" he asked. "The apothecary, who could back up what Ervan told you, is dead. Along with your friend. I am sorry about that, by the way. But we have to move forward. So what's the plan now?"

Belasko sighed, wiping tears from his eyes. "First, I have to go and sit vigil for Orren."

"Yes, of course," the Water King said, "but after that? What next?"

"After that..." Belasko looked up. "After that I break into the palace. It's the only way. If I can just see the king, tell him the truth... I might need your help."

The Water King's eyes gleamed as a grin spread across his face. "Break into the palace? The criminal in me can't resist a challenge like that. What do you need?"

Lilliana waited alone in the library, next to her old hiding place. Throughout her childhood Lilliana had told herself that she wasn't eavesdropping. She was just curious about what was going on in the world, about what her father did, about how their kingdom was run — and as people were so determined to treat her gently and insulate her from these truths, she needed to create her own opportunities to learn. That's all she was doing. Learning. Studying the art of ruling.

Today, however, she was eavesdropping.

Her father had all but cut himself off over the last few days, seeing few people, herself included, though she needed him after Kellan's murder. The only place he seemed to meet anyone was in his study. His private chambers had become a reclusive haven while he locked himself away and dealt with his grief. However, the kingdom still needed to be run. Decisions had to be made and orders given, so he met people in his private study for a few hours a day.

Lilliana made her way to the cupboard when she could, trying to gain an insight into what was going on in the kingdom, but also to hear her father's voice. She had missed it in the last few days.

Skirts bunched up around her, Lilliana sat on the floor in front of the cupboard. Its doors open, she placed her head inside, struggling against the confines of her clothes to get comfortable. If someone came into the library she knew she would look ridiculous but had placed a few tomes in the cupboard that she would claim to have been looking for. Hopefully her studious reputation would help carry off the deception.

Lilliana shifted slightly and grunted as a piece of corsetry poked her in the ribs. *Why don't men have to get trussed up like this? It's bloody unfair.*

She stilled herself as she heard the door close in the next room, the sound of murmured voices. They became louder as their owners moved into the room. She could easily make out her father's deep tones, but frowned to herself as she tried to place the other voice.

"How goes the search?" her father asked.

"We haven't found him yet, but we placed him at the docks just yesterday, where he narrowly missed being detained by the city watch. Belasko escaped, but his friend was killed." A memory tickled the back of her mind, but she still couldn't quite work out who it was.

"Orren? A shame. He was a good man. Had a family."

"Well he can't have been that good a man if he was helping a wanted criminal."

"He was loyal. A trait I thought you would admire, Inquisitor."

Something clicked into place. A memory of an inquisitor taking charge in the hours after her brother's death. Yes, she did recognise the voice. It was Inquisitor Ervan, the one in charge of investigating her brother's murder.

There was silence for a moment, before Ervan spoke again. "Loyalty I can admire, but to country. To the crown. Not to that dog, Belasko."

A pause before her father spoke. "Loyalty can make a man do strange things, whoever that loyalty is to. Belasko served me well for many years out of loyalty. To pursue him like this... I worry sometimes, Inquisitor, about what we are doing. What we have done."

"We do only that which is necessary, majesty."

Silence again. Her father sighed. "Yes, we do. Now leave me to my work. I have to make arrangements for my son's funeral. Come at once if you have more news about Belasko."

"Yes, majesty."

She heard Ervan's footsteps, then the door open and close. After a while, Lilliana could make out another sound.

Her father was crying.

13

Belasko was sweating, sinews straining and tired limbs aching as he tried to shift his bodyweight upwards, ever upwards.

I'll just walk in the front gates, that'll be easy. Idiot.

Things hadn't gone to plan. As he had got closer to the palace gates, Belasko had realised that they were not letting anyone enter with a raised hood. Everyone was being stopped and made to reveal their faces before they were allowed entry. Even though dusk was falling, there would be no way of hiding his face in the torchlight of the gate and square.

He turned and started to push against the tide of people.

"Oi, what are you doing? Don't fancy going in now?" asked one man who Belasko had to push past. "Or are you really ugly under that hood? Don't fancy showing your face."

"Not ugly — scarred," Belasko said. He held up an arm with freshly painted sores on it, done using the makeup Hibberth had given him. "Don't want to scare the kiddies."

The man paled and backed away. "Quite understandable. Here, let me get out of your way."

That was earlier. It was a good thing Belasko had come up with a back-up plan.

Less a plan, more a suicide attempt.

He thought back to earlier that day, when he and the Water King had been hatching their plans. "What do you need?" the crime lord had asked him.

"My first plan is simply to walk in the front gate during the guard changing ceremony. They always let the public in to watch that, even in times like this. Once I'm inside I can find a side door, slip into the outer palace and make my way through into the royal family's quarters."

"How are you going to manage that?" The Water King snorted. "They don't just leave the palace doors unlocked, never mind getting past all the guards. The place is no doubt teeming with soldiers at the moment. It sounds impossible to me."

"I have a way." Belasko thought of the master key that Lilliana had given him. "And I know the ins and outs of the palace, its corridors and quarters, better than most. Including a few paths known only to the royal family. Now, if that doesn't work..."

The Water King leaned forward. "Yes?"

"There is another way, but it's more difficult. And it might require your old smuggling skills."

"Oh ho, now I'm intrigued." The Water King laughed. "What is this more difficult way?"

So Belasko told him. The palace and its grounds, although grand, were of a higgledy-piggledy construction. As successive generations of monarchs and their favoured architects had added to the buildings and gardens — a new wing here, an ornamental hedge garden there — it led to some rather idiosyncratic design features. Particularly from a defensive point of view. Away from any of the main gates, original fortifications had been knocked down and expanded to include a small boating lake. There was a place where the walls turned back on themselves, forming a sort of chimney. It was a tight space, but someone with enough determination and skill could climb up to the corner where the walls met. Belasko had raised this as an issue with the palace guard a number of times. They had dismissed him, confident that the river would deter anyone foolhardy enough to attempt the climb; that it was far enough away from any of the bridges that connect the palace to the city; that the guards patrolling the walls passed by often enough that they'd spot someone climbing; that there would be few capable of attempting such a climb in the first place.

Belasko had disagreed. A determined climber could scale the walls undetected, if they waited for the guards to pass and slipped over after. It would be a while before anyone came by again.

Now I'm glad they didn't listen to me.

When his initial attempt to gain entry to the palace had failed, Belasko had returned across the bridge to meet Nobody and No One. They, in turn, ushered him away to meet other agents of the Water King, who took him to a riverside tavern in one of the less reputable parts of town. Part of the tavern was built out over the river, and Belasko was led down through the basement into a secret space below. There was a small dock built into a cave at the side of the river, hidden from prying eyes by a wall of rock. The narrow entrance wouldn't be visible from the opposite bank and left room for only a small rowboat to pass unobserved. One such was moored at the end of the dock, painted black and grey.

Waiting by the boat was the Water King, forgoing his usual exuberant clothing for more muted dull browns and greys. He saw Belasko appraising his attire and raised his eyebrows. "Wouldn't want to stand out against the water now, would I? The dark will only help us so much." He held out a sack to Belasko. "Here, some more suitable clothing for you as well. I made a guess about sizes." He gestured to the boat. "What do you think? Is she suitable?"

Belasko nodded, taking the sack from him. "Perfect. Did you get the weapons I asked you for?"

"Here, some from my personal armoury. Only the best for the royal champion." The Water King led him over to a table on which were laid out an array of weapons: knives of varying lengths, all manner of swords. Belasko surveyed them all, his eyes settling on a pair of lightly curved sabres. He reached out to touch their hilts.

"These are perfect."

The Water King cocked an eyebrow at him. "I thought you preferred a rapier?"

"For duelling. I'm proficient with just about any melee weapon you can name, and one should always use the right tool for the right job. I won't be duelling tonight. If I must fight it will likely be against multiple opponents at once as I try to find a way through to the king. I'll need to move through them quickly, making slashing cuts, not standing to fight toe to toe." A grim expression settled on his face. "I'll take a few of the knives as well."

They passed the time talking and playing cards, while Belasko's nerves and impatience built. Eventually it was deemed dark enough, and they made their way down to the dock.

Belasko climbed into the rowboat with the Water King and two other men, who remained silent. They were stocky, dressed in the same fashion as Belasko and the Water King, and they each took an oar. They looked to the Water King, who untied the boat and pushed them away from the dock. The rowers lowered their oars and, quickly and quietly, set them out of the little cave and into the swifter current of the river. Belasko could only admire their technique as the oars slid into the water seamlessly, silently, and powered them along.

The Water King leaned toward him. "Good, aren't they?" he whispered. "How are the clothes, by the way?"

"A surprisingly good fit," Belasko said. "You're wasted as a criminal. You'd have made an excellent tailor."

The Water King grinned and settled back. It looked as if Belasko had some luck left. A sea mist had rolled in from the Lan estuary and settled over the city. The fog would reduce visibility and muffle sound. The rowers' powerful strokes carried them along, following the instructions Belasko had given earlier, until eventually they reached the point where Belasko intended to make his climb. He signalled to the Water King and indicated where he wanted the boat to land. The Water King leaned over to the rowers and muttered something to them. They both nodded and carried on rowing.

Belasko frowned as they overshot the landing place. The reason was revealed when, after passing their target, they let the current of the river begin to carry them back. One of the rowers shipped their oar, the other left theirs trailing in the water, steering the boat into the bank beneath the palace walls as the current carried them gently. They bumped into the bank and one of the rowers and the Water King each reached out and placed a hand on the ground to hold the boat in position.

The Water King frowned up at the walls through the fog, the light from the torches placed at intervals along their top glowing in the misty air, but their light not reaching that far down the wall. He turned to Belasko. "Where are you going to climb?" he whispered.

Belasko pointed to an area of darkness. "Just there. It'll be tricky, but it's the only way."

The Water King's eyebrows shot up, disbelief writ clear across his face. "There?" He gestured at the wall. "You're going to climb up there?" When Belasko nodded, the disbelief was replaced by a look of wry humour. "I'm impressed. You're wasted as a duellist. You'd have made an excellent burglar. Now, on you go. Do you want us to wait here for you?"

Belasko climbed out of the boat. He looked up at the walls, then down to the Water King. He shook his head. "No. However this goes, I won't be going back this way."

"Good point. Well, I wish you the devil's own luck. You'll need it."

With no further words, the Water King released his hold on the bank and the rowers pushed them away into the river. Drifting, they let the current carry them away as silently as they had arrived. Belasko turned and made his way to the wall. He sighed. *Well, better get on with it.*

In truth, it would have been a difficult climb for Belasko in his prime. Now, with the years weighing on him, pain in his foot and joints, his ribs screaming in agony from the beating he had taken only days before, exhausted after the ordeals of the last few days, and with the walls made slick and damp by the fog that hid him from prying eyes, it should have been impossible. But he was determined, and the years of training he had put himself through gave him surprising reserves of strength and endurance. Belasko gritted his teeth against the pain and frustration, and pushed himself up the wall.

He was using both walls to climb, back pushed against one wall, feet against the other. He moved one foot until it was underneath his backside, leaving his other foot on the opposite section of wall. He pushed with the foot underneath him, lifting himself up the wall, using his hands as well. After moving up the wall he changed his leg positions and began again, wincing with pain every time he had to push off with his bad foot. It was painstaking and painful work, finger holds and toe holds as narrow and perilous as those of any free-climb in the mountains of his youth. But gradually he made his way up the wall. His borrowed swords, tied to his sword belt, dangled beneath him, his cloth bag hanging alongside them. He had taken the precaution of smearing the hilt of the swords, and anything else that might shine and catch the light and give away his position, with boot black.

Thank god it's a moonless night.

From above came the sound of footsteps, the clank of iron-shod spear butts on the ramparts, coming from two directions at once. Belasko stilled himself, knowing that even in this dark corner, movement could give him away. He wasn't yet in the light cast from the torches. Once he was, he had about ten minutes to get up, over the wall and away. He froze and, muscles twitching with the effort, held himself in place.

The two sets of guards exchanged a few words before they passed each other and continued on their way. Once he was sure they were gone, Belasko continued his climb.

Belasko heaved himself over the battlements, collapsing in an undignified heap on the other side. He lay there for a moment, gulping in air while his muscles shook from the strain, face and hair slick from the moisture in the night air that mingled with his sweat. Then he groaned, gritted his teeth, and forced himself to his feet.

To the nearest stairs and then down, into the palace grounds. From there I can make my way to the king's chambers — if I can avoid getting caught. I'd rather not have to fight my way through the palace. I'm not sure I'm up to it.

It took Belasko a moment to get his bearings. Then, limping, he set off for the nearest stairs.

Belasko crept through the palace grounds, repositioning the sabres on his sword belt as he went. In truth, only someone as knowledgeable as he, regarding the security arrangements and guard patterns in use at the palace, even stood a chance of making their way inside.

I'm surprised they haven't shaken things up. Did they not suspect I might try to get in to see the king?

There came the sound of murmured voices on the breeze.

Belasko froze behind an ornamental topiary that had been trimmed into the shape of a swan, pulling his dark robes about him. His hand crept to the repositioned sabres at his waist, though he was reluctant to draw and use them.

The voices resolved into a pair, male and female, that passed by the other side of the hedge. He heard a low murmur and delicate laughter, a rustle of clothing and a gasp of caught breath. There was silence for a little while, then the voices moved on.

Belasko waited for a few moments. From behind him he heard two splashes, then some high-pitched squealing followed by laughter. *Skinny dipping in the boating lake, on this cold night? They're brave.* He listened for a second, trying to hear if anyone else was approaching. Satisfied that he was now alone in this part of the gardens, he continued on his way.

The reason Belasko had chosen to scale the walls by the gardens was twofold. First, it was a climbable spot, if you were mad enough to try it. Second, Villanese kings and queens enjoyed private access to the gardens via a secret passageway that led from one of the pleasure gardens almost all the way to their private rooms and audience chamber. As well as affording them a private way in and out of the gardens, it was one of many escape routes built into the fabric of the palace by one or more of the king's paranoid ancestors. The passage was guarded at either end as a matter of course, and if Belasko were in charge that guard would have been increased. Fortunately for him, he wasn't in charge. If he had judged things correctly then the palace guard would have wanted not to intrude on the royal family during this time of grief, giving them as much space and privacy inside the palace itself as possible. Relying on the security of the palace walls to keep them safe.

If I'm right, they're bloody idiots. This is precisely the time that you need to surround the king and princess. Sod the niceties. It's a good thing for them it's me and not some assassin that walks these gardens tonight.

As he approached, Belasko could see the dim glow from the guards' covered lantern and began to make out the shape of the little guardhouse in the dark. It looked like nothing more than an innocuous stone hut, situated at the end of a low rise that ran back to the palace buildings proper. A casual observer would probably think it a folly, the sort of odd feature that the wealthy often sprinkled across their ornamental gardens. That casual observer might have wondered why there were two guards stationed in this apparent folly at every hour of the day and night. But then their attention would have been drawn to something else, some other feature of the garden designed to excite their senses, and they would have passed by without another thought.

Belasko knew different. He crept up to the low stone building, keeping to the deepest dark, and sidled up to the side wall, before creeping around to the front. He stopped to pick up a hefty stone, not wanting to alert the guards by drawing his swords, and he really didn't want to hurt them. At least, not permanently.

He waited, poised, breathing slowly, and listened to the sounds within the guardhouse. He heard laughter, swearing, the rattle of dice.

Belasko spun around the corner of the building and in through the open doorway. There were two guards inside, sat opposite each other on benches that were fixed to the walls. Neither was wearing their helmets but seemed to be using them to throw their dice into instead. They looked up at the intrusion. One started to rise, but before they could get to their feet Belasko struck, first to the left and then spinning to the right. The first guard collapsed, stunned, eyes rolled back in their head as Belasko's strike met its mark. The second guard grabbed his helmet from the floor and scrabbled backwards in their seat, bringing up the helmet to ward off Belasko's blow. Stone and helmet met with a metallic clunk and the helmet was knocked from the guard's grasp to rattle off the wall before landing on the ground. The guard, panicking now, fumbled to draw their sword and stand, tripping over their own helmet as it rolled across the floor, and they fell directly into Belasko's next blow. The second guard collapsed, stunned, to join the first.

Belasko winced at the trickle of blood that ran down the side of one guard's face. "Sorry, friend, that'll leave a mark. Hopefully the headaches will fade in a day or so. Although your punishment for letting me get the drop on you will be considerably longer."

He knelt by the guards and set to work tying their hands together with a short length of rope he produced from his bag. Belasko paused then, sighing. He took one of the guards' daggers and started to cut material from their surcoat.

"Sorry boys, I'm going to have to gag you. It won't do for you to start yelling for help if you wake up too soon."

Once he was satisfied the guards were securely tied, Belasko picked up their shuttered lantern from its place on the floor. He disturbed the pieces from the dice game in the process, as he trained its light on the back wall of the little guardhouse. Fixed to the rough stone wall were several rings, the sort you might tie a horse to. That casual observer might have thought these also out of place in a folly, but Belasko knew better. He frowned, trying to remember which ring was the right one. He reached out to the rightmost ring, tapping it with his finger. Belasko set down the lantern and, taking hold of the ring with both hands, gripped it tight and twisted.

At first it didn't budge and Belasko thought he had chosen wrong, but then it began to turn. There was a clunk behind the wall, then a click, and a line became apparent between the bricks. Belasko pulled, and the line spread, outlining the shape of a door. With a grating sound, a section of the wall swung outward to reveal a dark corridor behind.

Belasko knew from personal experience that the passage was long, so he checked the lantern to make sure its oil wouldn't run out, before stepping inside. He turned as he went, taking hold of a handle on the inside of the door and pulling it shut behind him. There was another grating sound, a click, a clunk, and then it was as if the door had never existed.

As Belasko walked, the faint sound of his footsteps echoed before and behind him. He sighed and trudged on. As he approached the end of the passageway, he shuttered the lantern completely. He eased up to the door, lifting up the rock he still carried. He used it to knock on the door, weakly tapping out the sign and countersign that indicated to those on the other side that it was safe to open up.

The door swung open slowly and Belasko took a step back into the darkness. One head and then another peered into the passage.

A female voice asked, "Garen? Marek? Is that you?"

With the light from beyond the doorway dazzling Belasko, he knew that the guards' eyes would take a while to adjust to the dark.

"We've both taken sick," he said, putting on a croaky voice. "You need to come now. I'm not sure he'll make it."

The guard spoke again. "This isn't the time for pranks."

"No prank," Belasko croaked. "Emergency. There's so much blood ..."

The two guards looked at each other, and one stepped into the passageway. "Alright, come into the light so we can see you. If you're both that ill you should be taken off duty."

The guard, squinting into the dark, was taken completely by surprise as Belasko's rock flew out of the darkness to hit him between the eyes. He fell, boneless, to the floor.

"Wha—" was all the other guard managed to say before

Belasko lunged out of the dark, grabbing her by the front of her surcoat and pulling her back into the passageway. There was a muffled yell and then silence. A few moments later, Belasko strode out of the passage and into the palace proper, closing the door behind him.

It took him a moment to find his bearings, but then he was off, stalking towards the royal apartments. The nearest way in was via the king's private audience chamber, which connected directly to his suite of rooms. It was only a little way down the corridor, and Belasko hoped he would make it at least that far before being discovered. He strode down the corridor, hood up. The corridors in this inner part of the palace were richly decorated, intricately carved, and inlaid wooden panels lined the walls. Expensive rugs covered the marble flooring and helped to muffle his footsteps.

If I walk confidently, as if I belong, I might not be noticed — despite my appearance. Hopefully I can hide in plain sight.

That hope was in vain. As he rounded a corner, Belasko came face to face with a group of three guards who halted in surprise.

"You. What are you doing here?" asked the leader, a sharp-featured older man with greying hair, as the other man and woman of the guard reached for their swords.

"I need to see the king," said Belasko. "I have information about the death of Prince Kellan."

The guards bristled at this, drawing their swords. "We don't just let anyone wander in off the street and talk to the king. How did you even get in here?" The leader frowned at Belasko, then peered past him down the corridor as if looking for the answer.

"I'm not just anyone. Forgive my appearance, it's been a trying few days." Belasko lowered his hood, shrugging off the cloak and letting it fall to the floor. "I have information for the king about Prince Kellan's real killer, and I must see him at once."

"Belasko!" The lead guard drew his sword. "The real killer? We're told it was you. And you think we'd let you in to see the king? You're liked by the Guard, Belasko, but this is a little much." He gestured at the swords Belasko wore. "Armed as well? Drop those. Make things easier on yourself, and we can get you back into the cell you somehow wriggled out of."

Belasko shook his head. "No. The last time I gave up my blade, I ended up being accused of a crime I didn't commit. I know who really arranged the prince's death and I must tell the king." He drew his swords. "Now let me by."

"Never," said the guardsman as he fell into the duelling stance known as The Honest Guard, from which most attacks could be readily countered. "Give yourself up."

"Never," said Belasko, "although you may surrender if you wish." In truth, Belasko had had enough of posturing. Although he had no desire to hurt these soldiers, he would not allow them to stop him.

He dashed forward, almost dancing between the guards, his swords a blur as he gave out a number of small wounds on his way past. Slashing cuts to a leg, a hand, an arm. He tried to hold back the full force of his blows, just wanting to slow them down, trusting in the medical care they would receive at their barracks to prevent any of the wounds having serious consequences.

Despite the injuries he had dealt them, the guards set off in pursuit, shouting the alarm as they went. "Danger! Intruder in the palace! Get the king to safety!"

Belasko rounded on the guards that pursued him, taking them by surprise. He used one of his swords to deflect a lunge towards the floor, using his opponent's momentum to draw them close enough to deliver a vicious blow to the nose with the hilt of the other sword that saw blood run. Eyes watering, his opponent staggered backwards, broken nose smeared across his face.

Belasko spun around a slash that came from his right, closing with the guard that had delivered it and crashing the pommel of one sabre into the guard's brow. She tumbled to the ground.

At last the leader came at him, more skilled than the others. Belasko parried his blows, waiting for his moment. The next time the guard swung, Belasko parried again, drawing his opponent's blade wide, then stepped in to deliver a mighty kick to the crotch. The guardsman fell to his knees, going pale, and Belasko left him behind, retching noisily.

He could hear shouts from down the corridor, but had reached his goal: the king's private audience chamber. He opened the door and stepped inside.

Belasko was now in the anteroom to the audience chamber. The doors to the chamber itself were directly opposite him, chairs lined up to either side along each wall for those waiting on his majesty's pleasure. There was a small table of dark polished wood in the centre of the room, a pair of heavy candlesticks upon it. He wasn't alone, for in that anteroom, as if waiting for him, was Ervan.

The inquisitor smiled his cold smile, standing up straight from where he had been leaning against the opposite door. "Hello Belasko," said Ervan. "This is a bold move on your part. When I heard the alarm raised, I thought it might be you. Didn't you wonder why security arrangements, the codes and countersigns, hadn't been changed since your escape? Why you had such an easy route into the palace?" He shook his head and laughed. "With your arrogance and penchant for bold moves, I thought you might try something like this. You've walked straight into the trap I set for you. I do hope you didn't injure any of the guards too badly." The inquisitor's one eye gleamed with curiosity. "Why have you come? What do you hope to accomplish?"

"I've come to tell the king the truth about you, how you had the prince poisoned."

Ervan tilted his head to one side. "You think that will do it, do you? Save your reputation, protect your life's work?"

Belasko shook his head. "It's not about my reputation. It's about justice. Seeing Kellan's killer brought to justice. Freeing a young woman whose only misfortune was to be a damn good cook and to catch my attention. Avenging Orren's death."

"You blame *me* for that?" Ervan's eyebrows rose towards the ceiling. He shrugged. "Well, I did tip the city watch off about the apothecary. After I killed him, of course. So I suppose I am at least partly culpable."

Belasko glared at the inquisitor. "Get out of my way, Ervan. You nearly did it. You nearly got away with it. But I'll see you dead for what you've done. I'll see you dragged before the court in chains."

Ervan grinned. "As much as I hate to deny you your public spectacle, I'm not letting you through this door. Why don't you lock the one behind you so we won't be interrupted? Then we can settle this as we should have done all those years ago."

Belasko reached behind him, feeling for the key in the door. He turned it, noting the satisfying clunk as the bolts slid home. He stepped further into the room, sheathing his left-hand sabre as he readied the other.

He shook his head. "You're mad. You couldn't have beaten me on your best day, when you still had both eyes."

Ervan pursed his lips and also stepped forwards, drawing his rapier. "I suppose you're right. Good thing for me that it's not your best day, eh?" He lunged at Belasko, and the fight began in earnest.

The inquisitor was right, it was far from Belasko's best day. He was exhausted, muscles aching and sore from his climb, suffering from his foot and aching joints, his bruises and the severe pain in his side. Ervan was a skilled opponent, despite lacking an eye. He was fresh to the fight, and that could be enough to make up for the difference in skill.

They traded blows as they moved around the room, each trying a score of attacks that the other easily countered. Back and forth they went, each probing the other's defences, each rebuffed. Then Belasko put his weight onto his bad foot. A flare of pain shot through him and he stumbled.

Ervan was on him, reeling off blow after blow, thrust after thrust, trying to capitalise on Belasko's misfortune, but the king's champion, still limping on his bad foot, met each attack head on despite the pain and his flagging strength.

After the flurry of attacks they both fell back, preserving their energies. Belasko had precious little left and couldn't waste it on a showy display, fighting with an economy of movement that might have appeared almost lazy to an outside observer, picking his moments to attack.

Ervan left him an opening, his sword held a little too wide, and Belasko pressed forward, lunging with a thrust that would have caught a less skilful opponent. Except it was a trap — a trap that, if Belasko were a little less tired, he would not have been lured into. As he lunged, Ervan pivoted to the side, grabbing Belasko's sword arm with his free hand and pulling him off balance. Ervan tried to bring his blade to bear on Belasko's back as he stumbled past, but the veteran duellist used his own momentum and bodyweight to carry himself past the inquisitor, spinning as he did so and twisting his arm free of Ervan's grip. His sabre opened a cut on Ervan's shoulder just as the inquisitor's scored a line of fire across his ribs. Both fell back panting, and started circling once more.

And so it went, the combatants more evenly matched than either would have thought, and before long both were bleeding from a number of cuts and wounds. It might have carried on like that for some time, had Belasko not seized an opportunity.

As they circled around the table in the centre of the room after another exchange of blows, Belasko, retreating, kept the table on Ervan's blind side. As they passed by it, Belasko stepped away and used the blade of his sabre to knock over the pair of heavy silver candlesticks. They teetered and fell onto Ervan, and he flinched at this unexpected touch from his blind side. The moment of hesitation was all Belasko needed. He knocked Ervan's blade to one side and lunged, the tip of his sabre burying itself in Ervan's one good eye and on through, into the brain beyond.

Ervan let out an odd, strangled sound and with an expression of utmost surprise on his face, dropped his sword. He fell to his knees, held up only by Belasko's blade. The swordsman raised his leg and pushed the inquisitor off his blade with his boot, Ervan's body slumping to the floor. He cleaned the sabre on Ervan's clothes before sheathing it, then turned to the door to the king's private audience chamber.

Belasko took a deep breath, trying to steady his rapidly beating heart, then put a hand to each door and pushed them open.

14

The doors opened with a crash. For a moment all was still, as if what Belasko saw was a tapestry or painting.

The audience chamber, although smaller and more intimate than the anteroom, was modelled on the throne room and was still a grand space by anyone's reckoning. It was richly furnished with expensive carpets and dark wood furniture, tapestries, pennants and mirrors hanging on the walls. It was a high-ceilinged chamber, lit in the day by tall stained glass windows and now, at night, by many candles — some in wall sconces, some on chandeliers that were suspended from the ceiling. The room was wider at the point where Belasko stood, narrowing towards a dais at the other end. Everything in the room was arranged to draw your attention towards that dais, on which was a finely carved wooden chair, a small throne for private occasions, which the king occupied. His daughter stood at his right shoulder, with a few courtiers beside her clad in their rich velvets and fine silks. Belasko was surprised to see that Aveyard, the Baskan ambassador, was among them in her uniform. They were all surrounded by a bristling complement of the royal guard, each of which had their blade drawn and levelled at Belasko's heart.

In that moment of stillness, Belasko looked up at Mallor, his king, who sat on his throne with a face like stone. Dark circles around his eyes, cheeks hollow, he looked drawn out by grief. Yet there was no give in him.

The poor man's not been eating. It was an odd thought to run through Belasko's mind, but he could not easily put aside the care he felt towards his king, his friend, no matter the situation.

There was silence in the room.

Belasko limped forwards, bowing towards the dais. "My king, there aren't words—"

"You're right about that, traitor." The king spat his words, harsh, angry. He roared the next, standing from his throne. "How dare you? How dare you come into my home? You, who murdered my son, abused all trust given to you, you—"

"Forgive me for interrupting, my king, but I did not kill Prince Kellan. I loved him well, as you know, and swore to protect him as I protect you and all of your line."

The king settled back onto his throne, gently pulled by Lilliana's hand on his shoulder. Her touch seemed to calm him, though he still glowered at Belasko. "Alright. I'll entertain this fanciful notion for a moment, before the guards here cut you to pieces. Even you cannot stand against so many." The king wiped his hand across his eyes, suddenly weary. "If you didn't poison my son, who did?"

Belasko stepped further into the room, ignoring the drawn swords, addressing only the king. "Ervan, your majesty. The inquisitor who led the investigation into Kellan's death. He confessed as much to me when he had me prisoner down by the docks just yesterday. He purchased a poison from an apothecary who owed him a favour, then got a kitchen boy to drop it into the prince's food, under the guise of playing a prank on Kendra, the cook I had helped to find employment in the kitchens."

The king gestured towards the anteroom behind Belasko. "And where is this kitchen boy you say poisoned the food? It could easily have been the other cook you mentioned, under your own instigation. Where is the apothecary?"

Belasko shook his head. "Both dead, majesty. Ervan had the boy killed, under the guise of catching an illness in the cells, and he got to the apothecary before I could and had him killed as well. He's been covering up his tracks and using me to take the blame. He hated me, for the loss of his eye in a fencing accident when we were younger, and for being what I am: a peasant who has risen, in his opinion, too far."

"If you are to be believed, then the black-clad corpse on the floor in there means you have just killed the one man who could corroborate what you say." The king gave a bitter laugh. "Oh Belasko, don't you see? You claim that Ervan has been going around killing people to cover his tracks, when it could just as easily have been you covering yours. Weren't you surprised at an apothecary's shop just the other night? Your friend Orren killed in the act of helping you? Your actions tonight show someone desperate to cover up the truth rather than reveal it. Why should we trust you, when you come in the night dressed like a burglar? Ervan was loyal, almost obsessively so. Why would he kill my son?"

"*Because* he was loyal. To you, and to the throne — not to Kellan. He thought Kellan wasn't a suitable heir. He was fanatically loyal to you..." Belasko paused, frowning. "This is where it doesn't make sense."

The king laughed again. "Oh, *here* is where it doesn't make sense?"

Belasko shook his head. "You're right, majesty. Ervan was obsessively loyal to you. Why would he do anything that would hurt you... unless it was in your interest?"

The silence in the audience chamber was deathly. All eyes were on Belasko.

"He said to me, when he was gloating and thought I was soon to die, that Kellan wasn't fit to rule. That he was a drunk and a wastrel. Complained that he spent his evenings carousing. Whoring. In and out of the worst parts of the city. He said that Princess Lilliana was the better choice as heir."

The king remained silent, glowering at Belasko, who peered up at him with a quizzical expression. "I hadn't thought about it until now — I've been too busy just staying alive — but his words... they echoed almost exactly someone else. They're your words. You said them to me the night we went to the Golden Hind. Almost exactly the same. Why would he kill Prince Kellan unless he knew that it was something that you wanted? That you... ordered?"

There were gasps from the others in the room. Shock on every face — except Ambassador Aveyard's. Instead, her face wore an expression of realisation that settled into one of relief. The silence was broken as people began to shout that it wasn't so, couldn't be so. But Belasko could only stare up at his king, a feeling of horror blooming in his chest. Lilliana stared at her father, a stricken look on her face.

Belasko looked up at the king as argument raged around him; looked at the hurt on Lilliana's face. And he knew. He knew that what he had said was true.

"Silence!" roared the king. "Silence! Guards, seize that man and silence him at once. We'll have no more of his lies spun in this room." He laughed. "Me, have my own son killed? What a ridiculous idea. All know how I have grieved my son's death. All know how much I loved him."

"Yes, we do, Father." Lilliana stepped out from behind the throne. "I know how much you loved him, how much you love me, but I also know how much you love our country. Its security, and the security of the succession, has ever been your most solemn duty. I know how you have been grieving, not just because I have been grieving too, but because I have heard your sobs."

The king looked up at his daughter, face pale and taut with emotion.

"I heard your sobs in your study, and much else besides. Because you shut me out, I found other ways to listen. I heard you with Ervan. I remember your exact words, which only make sense to me now. 'Loyalty can make a man do strange things,' you said. 'Whatever or whoever that loyalty is to. I worry sometimes, Inquisitor, about what we are doing. What we have done.' Your words Father, and then you cried. I could hear it. But now I know, they weren't just tears of grief, but of guilt. You had my brother killed." Belasko stared at Lilliana, who looked at her father, her heartbreak visible in her eyes. "How could you do it, Father? Kellan loved you. All he wanted was to make you proud."

King Mallor seemed to sink then, as if deflated. "Make me proud? Proud of what, his chasing after whores? His prowess at drinking and pissing the country's money up the wall?" He shook his head. "Kellan was too weak, had too many flaws that our enemies would have exploited had he ever become king. I loved my son, but he was a good-for-nothing wastrel."

The sound of the slap echoed across the room. Lilliana cradled her hand as a red mark spread over her father's cheek "He was only like that because he was bored. If you'd given him something to do, trusted him, he wouldn't have done those things. All he wanted was to prove himself, but you never gave him the opportunity."

The king blinked, raising a hand to his cheek as he stared at his daughter in surprise. Then in anger. Guards hovered, hesitant, their training demanding that they intervene with a threat to their king warring with their reluctance to act against the princess. King Mallor sat straighter on his throne. "He never earned the opportunity. He never behaved in a way that befit his birth right. Do you think it is easy, child? To sit on the throne? To make the hard decisions, choose the path that must be taken, no matter the cost? That is what it means to rule. You must put the important before the personal, set your feelings to one side, and govern by what is best for the kingdom. Our people need a good heir, one who can be trusted to do their duty. And so I give them you."

"Don't you dare," Lilliana hissed. "Don't you dare pretend you did this for the good of the kingdom. Whatever reasons you had, I don't understand them. I won't understand them."

"Well then, we are at an impasse. How shall we decide who is right?"

"There is no impasse, Father. No one here thinks you are right. Whatever else you have done, you have broken the laws of the kingdom, conspired to murder. No matter your reasons or who you are, the law holds."

The king nodded, a sad expression on his face. "Perhaps you are right. If the law holds, then our oldest law holds too. That of trial by combat. Shall we turn to the old ways daughter, to decide? I challenge you, or your champion, to trial by combat, to prove that I am in the right. Who will stand for you?"

"I will," said Belasko, as all eyes turned back to him. "I will stand for the princess."

Mallor snorted. "You, Belasko? You look like you're about to fall down."

"Nevertheless, I stand. Your highness, will you accept me as your champion?"

Lilliana gathered herself, standing up straight and thrusting her chin out. "I do, Belasko, thank you."

"Well," said the king, "your little treachery is complete. Who, then, will stand for me?"

Silence. The king looked around the room, but none of

those assembled would meet his eye. Angry now, he asked again, "Who will stand for me?"

An officer of the guard that Belasko recognised stepped forward. "I will not stand for you, but I will lend you my sword," said Majel.

The king looked stricken. "Will none of you stand for your king?"

"Kellan was well loved by the guard, King Mallor, something you would have done well to remember before confessing to having him murdered before a room full of them," said Belasko. "And you know the law as well as I. You issued the challenge, you must be prepared to back it up. If none will stand for you, then you stand alone. In the duelling circle. With me. Majel, pass me your dagger."

The guardswoman obliged, and Belasko paced out the duelling circle, scratching a line in the inlaid wooden floor as he went. He passed the dagger back to Majel. "Sorry if that's blunted the edge." He frowned. "If it's to be a duel then we should do this properly, someone fetch me Ervan's rapier. Your majesty, if we are following the old ways we would both strip to the waist, but I think getting down to our shirtsleeves should be sufficient." He removed the jacket the Water King had given him and, folding it neatly, placed it outside the circle before rolling up his shirtsleeves. Then he undid his sword belt and passed it to Majel. "Would you mind these for me? They're borrowed from a friend." She nodded and stepped back as another guard, a confused look on his face, handed him Ervan's rapier. Belasko took a moment to find the balance of the sword, swinging it back and forth. Then he stepped into the circle and turned to face the king.

"I await your majesty's pleasure."

The king was silent for a moment, before he started pulling at the fastenings of his richly brocaded doublet. He yanked savagely at the buttons and ties, heedless to the sound of tearing cloth and delicate mother of pearl buttons that fell to the floor. Mallor threw the doublet over the arm of his carved wooden throne and held his hand out to Majel. "I made this bed, I might as well lie in it." Majel passed over her sword, a rapier of the sort Belasko favoured for duelling, handle first. The king took a moment to feel the weight of it, giving a few practice swings. "It's been a while since I held a blade."

He stepped into the circle. The two combatants circled each other, wary.

"Why?" Belasko asked.

King Mallor lunged at him. It was a clumsy attack and Belasko sidestepped it without even raising his blade.

"Why?"

Another lunge. This time Belasko batted the blow away angrily.

"Why?"

"Goddamn it, you know why. Kellan wasn't fit to rule. It needed to be done."

Lunge. Belasko parried and riposted, leaving a line of blood across the king's cheek.

"No, it didn't. You didn't see the promise that Kellan had within him."

"Shut up."

Another lunge, parried and riposted. A line of blood appeared on the king's other cheek to match the first.

"Pinning the blame on me, that hurt. I served you loyally all these years. I even thought we were friends."

Mallor snorted. "Friends? I like you well enough Belasko, but you're a peasant. We were never — could never — be friends. Your life was sworn in service to me to be used as I saw fit. You have always been a tool for my use, a tool that has outlived its usefulness. With your body failing, your ability to be my champion waning, I decided that you could serve me in this one last thing. Why couldn't you just do what was needed?"

"Oh, I have done what was needed. Now why don't you try me properly and see if my abilities are waning?"

The king roared, charging at Belasko across the circle. Belasko stepped out of his way, delivering a cut to the back of King Mallor's leg as he passed that made him stagger. Limping now, the king turned back to face Belasko. "Come on you coward, kill me. Stop toying with me and strike me down, great duellist."

Belasko shook his head. "This brings me no pleasure, your majesty. I have protected you these many years. But while you have sworn to do what you think is necessary, I am sworn to do what is right. To uphold the laws of our kingdom and protect the royal family from threats. No matter the cost. You are now one of those threats, and for what you've done, for the lives your actions have cost, I will kill you, though it pains me to do so. Let us continue your fencing lesson. Your first attack was poor, would you like to try again?"

Mallor staggered forwards in an attempt at a lunge, this time Belasko didn't even move his feet. He deflected the king's blow, thrust the point of his own sword into the meat of the thigh on Mallor's remaining good leg, eliciting a howl of pain from the monarch, and returning to the en guard position.

"Really, I'd expect better. Again."

Mallor aimed a wild swipe at Belasko's head, bringing his sword around from the right, which the duellist ducked under. He pushed the king's arm as it went by, causing the king to overbalance and fall to the side. As the king twisted around Belasko used the edge of his own blade to score a deep cut along his side, the rapier slicing through the king's fine linen shirt as if it were paper.

The king turned back to him, teeth gritted against the pain.

"Again."

Mallor growled, aiming a vicious backhand blow at Belasko, which he leaned back to avoid, the tip of the king's blade whistling passed his face. The king's own momentum pulled him off balance and Belasko stepped into him, bringing the hilt of his sword crashing into Mallor's face. The king staggered back, spitting blood and teeth, a look of fury in his eyes. He was tiring now, bleeding from the wounds that Belasko had inflicted. He roared defiance and threw himself at Belasko in one last desperate attack, making no attempt at defence. Quicker than thought, a lifetime of training and honed reflexes at work, Belasko deflected the attack and brought his blade back to bear on the king. The sheer momentum of the king's attack carried him onto Belasko's blade and it took little effort from the swordsman to run him through.

The king's sword dropped to the floor as he brought his hands to clutch at the blade that pierced his body, heedless of how that blade cut into his fingers. His mouth opened and closed as blood ran out of him and onto the floor, seemingly disbelieving that he had been killed. As the light left the king's eyes Belasko let go of his blade, letting it fall with the king's body. A pool of blood spread around the twitching remains of what had been the ruler of Villan.

Belasko looked over to Lilliana, tears in both their eyes. "The king is dead," he whispered, "long live the queen."

15

Kendra sat in her cell, trying to read by the dim torchlight. She heard the clank of bolts sliding in the door at the end of the corridor and set her book down, standing and smoothing out her skirts. Two sets of footsteps made their way down to her cell.

"A bit late for dinner, aren't we? I thought you'd forgotten me for a..." She trailed off. The two people that now stood in front of her cell were the last that she had expected to see.

Princess Lilliana and Belasko both looked sad and tired. Belasko was swinging a set of keys around his finger.

"Sorry for the delay," said the princess. "Shall we get you out of here?"

Belasko unlocked her cell door and swung it open.

"I-I don't understand," said Kendra. "What's happened? Belasko, how are you here? You look awful, by the way." Which was true. The swordsman looked exhausted and filthy, face a riot of bruises and swelling, moving as if he was in pain. She could see that he wore bandages in several places.

He laughed. "Good, then my appearance matches how I

feel. As to what's happened," The swordsman raised his eyebrows, "that's a long story."

"Well, give me the short version. How are you here and setting me free?"

A sad look crossed Belasko's weary face. "The short version is that I found out who actually killed Prince Kellan. It was Inquisitor Ervan. I broke into the palace to tell the king, except he already knew. He'd planned the whole thing."

"What?" Kendra said, shocked. "The king had Kellan…?"

"Killed," said Lilliana.

It was only then that Kendra realised that what she had at first taken as weariness was grief, weighing heavily upon them both. "Oh, your highness," she said. "I'm so sorry. I can't — I mean, there aren't words…"

Lilliana smiled at her. "Thank you, that's kind of you."

"But what happened then? Where is the king?"

"He is dead, his scheme exposed. Which means that you're free to go. I'm hoping that, after some time off to spend with your family and recuperate from what has happened, you'll come back to us here at the palace. Resume your duties in the kitchens."

"I don't know. The job hasn't exactly gone as I'd expected."

Lilliana gave her a sad smile. "I imagine not. Well, there is definitely some compensation due, and I think a substantial pay rise as well. Now come out of there, I've got a carriage ready to take you to your father's inn. Think on it. I'll send someone to see you in a few days and you can discuss it then."

"For my part, I'm sorry that you got caught up in this whole mess," said Belasko. "I feel responsible, having brought you into the palace. I'll do what I can to find a way to make it up to you. Now," Belasko gestured at the still open cell door, "come on. Your freedom awaits."

~

It was later that night, much later, and they were sat in a small lounge attached to Lilliana's rooms, each nursing a steaming cup of tea. The new queen blew on hers to cool it, then looked up at Belasko. "What I don't understand is how you managed all this. To avoid the city watch, the Inquisition, make your way into the palace. All alone, against everything."

"I wasn't entirely alone. I had some help from..." Belasko smiled, "unexpected quarters."

"You'll have to tell me about that."

"Someday, perhaps. Although I have promised my discretion. Let's just say I owe some people some very large debts. You will also want to make some amendments to the palace's security arrangements. Once word gets out that I scaled the walls others will figure out how it was done." His smile became a frown as he thought of those who had assisted him. "You may also want to place extra guards on the royal jewel house."

Lilliana raised an eyebrow at that and, after a moment of uneasy silence had passed, gave a smile of her own. "I have something for you." She set down her tea and, standing, went to a small writing desk in the corner of the room. She opened a drawer and removed a folded piece of paper, which she passed to Belasko. "Here. The letter to my father which Ervan claimed as evidence of your guilt. I, um, removed it from my father's study a few days ago. There's something wrong with it. What do you see?"

Belasko put down his tea cup and held the letter up to the light. He frowned as he examined it. "Well, this is my seal." He thumbed the broken wax on the outside of the letter. "And this is my signature. But the rest of it?" He bent his head to read the letter's contents. "It goes on about my guilt, and how I have only acted for the good of the kingdom. It... it makes the same justifications your father and Ervan did. Begs your father to forgive me for Prince Kellan's death. In all honesty, it reads like the work of an unhinged mind. But apart from the signature, and the address on the outside of the letter, none of this is my handwriting. How have they managed that?"

Lilliana held out her hand. "May I?" He passed the letter back and she examined it. "That was my own thinking. I've had letters from you myself and recognised that it isn't your handwriting on the letter. Perhaps... I've read of certain compounds that, when made up, can leach the ink from paper, removing the original message. I've read of it but never seen it done. However—" She moved back to the writing desk, picking up a small charcoal drawing stick. Placing the letter on the desk she began to rub the charcoal lightly across it. "—even if they removed the ink, they wouldn't have been able to remove the impressions you made when you first wrote the letter. Ah, yes, here we go. Take another look." She passed the letter back to Belasko and he read it again.

Under the faint darkening where she had deftly applied the charcoal, he could make out clear lines where what had been written previously was now visible.

"See?" She smirked as she retook her seat, carelessly wiping the charcoal on her hands onto the arms of her chair. "Not just a pretty princess." The smirk fell from her face. "Or queen now, I suppose."

Well, I'll be...

"This is a letter I wrote your father last year, asking his permission to let me acquire more land for my Academy. It makes me wonder, how long had they been planning all this? Was anyone else in on it, staff or servants, or did your father and Ervan act alone?"

"Questions I am now asking myself, answers to which I will start seeking in the morning. Several members of the palace staff seem to have fled since the events in the audience chamber — including my father's old steward, Viktor.

Remember him? It was his key that helped in your escape, right at the start of all this. There are already people out looking for them, but that is tomorrow's worry. What about you, Belasko? Now you have got to the truth, exposed Kellan's killers, avenged your friends and thrown the kingdom into further disarray." Her smile took any sting out of the last words. "What are you going to do now?"

"Now?" Belasko took a sip of his tea. "Sleep for a thousand years. At least, that's what I'd like to do. If I can stay here in the palace tonight, then tomorrow I'll go to my house in the city and gather some things. Then I must return to my academy. There is much to do, much to put right. I have to see Orren's family, tell them what happened. Then there will be a funeral to organise."

"More than one. We haven't even buried my brother yet. Now we'll have to organise something for Father as well. Quite what, I don't know. I'm sorry for your loss, by the way. Orren. I didn't know him well, but what I knew of him I liked."

Belasko smiled, looking down at his cup. "He was a good man. My best friend. The heart of a lion and the head of an ox. I loved him and miss him now, more than I can say."

Lilliana met his eyes as he looked back up, an inquisitive look on her face. "Forgive me the personal question, Belasko, but Orren married and had a family. Plenty of soldiers do. Why didn't you?"

Belasko coughed, clearing his throat. "Why didn't I?" He shook his head. "I loved someone, once, if you must know. They didn't return my feelings, couldn't return them. There were others, but when I became a duellist, the royal champion, I knew that I would likely die sooner rather than later. While death is a possibility for a soldier, it's a certainty for a duellist. I didn't want to burden a partner with that knowledge, and the eventual aftermath. I'm as surprised as anyone else to find myself still standing all these years later. Instead, my duties became my focus. And so they must again. There is much to do. This time, when I return to my Academy, I'm not sure I'll be coming back to the city."

Lilliana observed him over the rim of her teacup, saying nothing. Belasko continued.

"Your majesty, I've been thinking... That is to say, the events of the last few days, your father's betrayal. The loss of my best friend. And tonight, killing the man I dedicated my life to protecting... There are many injuries, not just physical, that need to heal." He shook his head. "I think I've had enough of the machinations of palace life, of intrigue and danger. Of being used as a pawn in a political game." He paused, surprised at the bitterness in his own voice. "I'm sorry, my queen. It's time I retired to my Academy, gave my students the attention they deserve. I'll find you a proper champion, not one whose best days are behind him."

Lilliana sat for a moment, letting his words settle. Then she nodded. "I think that's for the best. Don't misunderstand me, I'm grateful for what you've done. But your actions have shone light into a dark place and it will take time to recover. The people have been told for days now that you killed my brother and many will not trust you. I will make sure that the truth is known, but it will take time to sort out the mess of all that's happened and get that truth out. I also have to stand on my own for a while, be seen to be independent, the leader my people need. If you were to stay, people might say that you were influencing me. There have already been whispers tonight, in these scant few hours, that you mean to marry me and take the crown for yourself. As if I have no say in the matter! I—"

Belasko gave a bitter laugh, causing Lilliana's eyebrows to rise. "I'm sorry, your majesty, but they're definitely barking up the wrong tree there. I'm, um... *otherwise* inclined. Something that your father knew, but isn't open knowledge at court."

Lilliana flushed. "Oh, I see. That's not all that uncommon.

Still, rumours persist and spread faster than they can be stopped, no matter the truth of things. I intend no offence, but when I do marry I would prefer someone closer to myself in age."

"No offence taken." Belasko smiled. "I would wish that for you myself."

Queen Lilliana's face took on a more serious cast. "Also, speaking personally, for all that he did, my father was still my father, and having him killed in front of me, by someone I've known since childhood..." She paused, coughing as she dashed away sudden tears with the back of her hand. "I'm not sure how comfortable I am having his killer at court, no matter the debt I owe him. I'm sorry Belasko, but I can't have you here. I can't be seen to have you here. Not now. Maybe not ever."

He swallowed, surprised at the lump in his throat. "This is it, then. My time as the royal champion is over."

Lilliana shook her head. "No, not just yet. Not until you've found your replacement. Go to your Academy, but be ready should I need you. I know — I trust — that you will always do your duty."

As Belasko set down his cup and saucer they rattled slightly, his hands shaking. He stood, wincing against the pain of the injuries he had sustained that night and the nights before, and looked down at Lilliana. Grieving. In pain. Every inch a queen.

"You know me too well, majesty." He saluted. "Until you need me, then. Farewell." With that he turned on his heel and, without looking back, left the room.

THE END

If you want to see what's next for Belasko book two of *The Royal Champion, The Swordsman's Descent*, is available now!

AFTERWORD

Belasko will return! The Swordsman's Descent, book two of The Royal Champion series, is out now.

If you've enjoyed this adventure and would like to be kept up to date with my news (as well as receiving a free ebook of *The Swordsman's Intent*, the prequel novella set 15 years before *The Swordsman's Lament,* short stories and exclusive content) then make sure to sign up to my newsletter at gmwhite.co.uk.

BY THE AUTHOR

The Royal Champion Series:
Prequel Novella: The Swordsman's Intent
Book One: The Swordsman's Lament
Book Two: The Swordsman's Descent

ABOUT THE AUTHOR

G.M. White has always been an avid reader, a love of the written word instilled in him by his parents at an early age. This may or may not have something to do with the fact that he was a very talkative child and the only time he was quiet was when he had his head in a book. Anyway, we'll give them the benefit of the doubt on that one.

A lifelong storyteller, he finally decided to put his imagination to good use and set pen to paper (well, fingers to keyboard) and started to write down the worlds that he carried with him in his head. The Swordsman's Lament is his first novel.

A reformed Londoner, he now lives on St Martin's in the Isles of Scilly.

ACKNOWLEDGMENTS

There are so many people to thank, for their help, support, and inspiration. Too many to mention them all here, so here are the highlights. My wife Charlie, without whose love and support none of this would be possible, and who drives me to improve every day. My Mum and Dad, who gave me my love of the written word and always encouraged me to follow my dreams. My brother Steve, who is always the first to read what I have written and is incredibly enthusiastic and brimming with ideas, and my aunt Carole, who has always encouraged me to pursue my creative endeavours. The friends who took in their stride my desire to write a novel and gave their support. My editor, Vicky Brewster, who helped me to uncover the story I wanted to tell even when it was hidden under those early drafts. Tad Williams, who isn't just a legendary author in the field of speculative fiction but has, over the last few years, taken the time to answer a fledgling author's questions with real thought and consideration. Mark Stay and Mark Desvaux of the Bestseller Experiment podcast for providing a treasure trove of information for aspiring authors, indie or otherwise, which helped to give me the confidence to write and publish this book. Also the BXP Team, the community that has grown around that podcast, for their support, brainstorming prowess, and feedback on such things as blurbs and cover design. Special mention goes to Julian Barr, for very kindly reading an early draft of this text and offering very helpful feedback. Writers' HQ, another fabulous writing community, whose courses and online writing group helped me develop this novel from an idea, to an outline, to a completed first draft. Last, but not least, my colleagues at Churchtown Farm, for letting me witter on at length about writing and taking an interest.

www.ingramcontent.com/pod-product-compliance
Lightning Source LLC
Chambersburg PA
CBHW030338310726
48979CB00001B/82
* 9 7 8 1 9 1 6 1 7 9 9 6 7 *